"I'm sure we can negotiate something."

"Negotiate...?" Kate parroted.

"Negotiation...I want something, you want something, we come to a mutually beneficial arrangement," Javier elucidated slowly in his rich drawl.

"What do I have that you want?" Kate quavered, wrapping her arms protectively across her chest.

"I need to get married."

KIM LAWRENCE lives on a farm in rural Anglesey, Wales. She runs two miles daily and finds this an excellent opportunity to unwind and seek inspiration for her writing! It also helps her keep up with her husband, two active sons and the various stray animals which have adopted them. Always a fanatical consumer of fiction, she is now equally enthusiastic about writing. She loves a happy ending!

THE
BLACKMAILED
BRIDE

KIM LAWRENCE

BLACKMAIL BRIDES

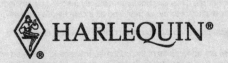 HARLEQUIN®

TORONTO • NEW YORK • LONDON
AMSTERDAM • PARIS • SYDNEY • HAMBURG
STOCKHOLM • ATHENS • TOKYO • MILAN • MADRID
PRAGUE • WARSAW • BUDAPEST • AUCKLAND

ISBN 0-373-82032-1

THE BLACKMAILED BRIDE

First North American Publication 2006.

Copyright © 2002 by Kim Lawrence.

This edition published by arrangement with Harlequin Books S.A.

® and TM are trademarks of the publisher. Trademarks indicated with ® are registered in the United States Patent and Trademark Office, the Canadian Trade Marks Office and in other countries.

www.eHarlequin.com

Printed in U.S.A.

CHAPTER ONE

JAVIER drove through the large ornate gates and up the long winding driveway lined with olive trees towards the distinctive Moorish tower that stood against the backdrop of the mountains. He pulled the Mercedes he was driving in a space beside a battered Beetle which stood out like a sore thumb amongst the other expensive models.

So, Serge still hadn't persuaded Sarah to part with her old car. An easy-going young woman who would, as a rule, do anything for her husband, Sarah did have a few blind spots.

Javier himself was unmarried, but did not lack female companionship. It had never required much, if any, effort on his part to have attractive women hanging on his every word, but no special woman had ever materialised from these adoring masses. The possibility that if and when he discovered her she wouldn't be interested had simply not crossed his mind!

Then he'd met Sarah.

Now he was thirty-two, didn't take *anything* for granted, and was, he liked to think, more discerning about women—*too* damned discerning, according to his grandfather, who wanted his chosen heir safely married.

Javier could have taken the easy option and chosen a suitable consort, a woman from a background similar to his own that would enable her to cope with the pressures of being a member of one of the wealthiest families in Europe, just as his father before him had. That was the problem, everytime he was tempted to take the easy way out Javier was confronted by the spectre of his parents' disastrous union.

Before he'd left the family estate in Andalucia to make the journey to Majorca the old man had finally issued an ultimatum.

'Marry before I die or I'll leave everything to Raul or one of the others!' Felipe Montero had warned his favourite grandson dramatically.

Javier's immediate reaction to this not very subtle blackmail had been anger; did his grandfather know him so little that he imagined he could be bought...?

He turned to Felipe with much of the pride and hauteur his grandfather was famed for etched on his own chiselled features. What he saw in the old man's lined face made him bite back the caustic response hovering on his tongue.

Javier had no illusions about what his grandfather was capable of. Felipe Montero was devious, he frequently bullied and connived, he routinely plotted and schemed—in short, when it came to getting his own way he was capable of acts of great ruthlessness. However he was never crude in his manipulations and, even more significantly, Javier had never seen his grandfather look frightened before!

'You'll live a long time yet...?'

Felipe smiled; Javier had never needed things spelled out. He was a sharp judge of character who read people almost as well as he read the financial markets.

'No, as a matter of fact I won't. The doctors give me six months at the outside.'

Javier didn't tell Felipe that this wasn't possible, he didn't scream, as people often did when they were confronted with the mortality of someone they couldn't imagine life without, that the doctors *must* be able to do something.

He wanted to, but he didn't.

Instead after a short pause he nodded, not insulting his grandfather by questioning the grim prognosis.

'What is it?'

'Cancer. The damned thing's spread from my lungs. So there's not much point packing these things in,' Felipe observed with a deep throaty chuckle as he inhaled deeply on his cheroot. 'And don't tell anyone else yet—*nobody*. If the news gets out millions will be wiped off the value of the company…' A flicker of revulsion appeared in the older man's eyes. 'And I don't doubt they'll all start treating me as if I'm in my dotage,' he added, a tremor in his deep voice. It wasn't dying but the manner of it that scared Felipe Montero.

'No one will do that.'

A silent promise was exchanged in the look that passed between the two men.

Felipe sighed, satisfied. 'Unfortunately this couldn't come at a worst time, of course, with the Brussels deal…'

An extremely disciplined man, it wasn't often that Javier's emotions got the better of him, but as he listened to his grandfather fret about the fate of the financial empire he'd expanded up over his lifetime something snapped.

'There is such a thing as a good time to die?' he gritted. 'To hell with the company!' His deep voice cracked. 'You're going to *die,* Grandfather.'

'We're all going to die,' came the careless response. 'If you really care,' Felipe goaded slyly, 'show it. Marry Aria…she loves you.'

A wry laugh was wrenched from Javier. 'You never give up, do you?'

If and when he did marry, Javier knew it wouldn't be to someone who loved him, someone he might hurt as his father had his mother. A fragile creature, his mother had never grasped the fact she was meant to turn a blind eye to her husband's mistresses; she was meant to look attractive, bring up their son and be the perfect hostess.

'This is no laughing matter, Javier,' the old man reproached sternly. 'Continuity, blood lines are important; you need sons.'

'I'm sorry, but I can't.'

The idea of losing his inheritance didn't frighten Javier. He immediately recognised that there was part of him that might actually welcome the situation. A man who needed the constant buzz of physical and mental challenges, he could think of few things more exciting than the challenge of starting from scratch, and few things more satisfying than knowing at the end of the day that everything you'd achieved was down to your own efforts, nothing to do with being born into a wealthy dynasty.

Wealth brought its privileges, but Javier had been raised to believe it also carried responsibilities. His deeply ingrained sense of family duty would never allow him to do anything more than occasionally dream about the luxury of being a free agent.

Deep down, however, he was pretty sure it wouldn't come to that, his grandfather would never disinherit him for standing his ground. Nothing in his manner even hinted at this belief. He couldn't do much for his grandfather but he could at least let Felipe play the heartless tyrant he liked the world to see him as.

Felipe searched his grandson's unyielding face with growing frustration. 'This is about that silly blonde you let Serge snatch right from under your nose, I suppose… Don't look so stunned, boy.' He laughed. 'Do you think I'm blind? If you want my opinion, she'd have been a disastrous match for you…'

Javier swallowed his anger with difficulty.

'…Far too sweet and malleable. You need someone with a bit more fire…'

'Like *Aria*,' Javier cut in drily.

Felipe conceded this point with a grunt. 'Well, it doesn't *have* to be her…but if you want to be my heir you'll marry someone and soon…'

'We shouldn't be arguing…not now…'

'Why change the habit of a lifetime? If you start agreeing with me the family will know something's wrong straight away, and I won't be able to move for everyone being *nice* to me,' he observed with a shudder.

When two people who were congenitally incapable of compromise worked together there were bound to be some sparks. Javier's combustible relationship with his grandfather was not without its moments of conflict, often vocal conflict, at least on Felipe's side—Javier was more inclined to smouldering silences. Javier knew his rivals within the family frequently crossed their fingers and hoped he'd overstep the mark one day and alienate the old man totally. What they failed to understand was the deep mutual respect the warring parties felt for each other.

'I'm sorry.'

'You're a stubborn idiot!' the old man railed at his tall grandson's retreating back.

A man with extraordinary self-discipline, Javier pushed aside the personal issues that filled his mind as he stepped out of the air-conditioned luxury of his Mercedes. He barely registered the blast of baking heat which immediately hit him; Majorca had been experiencing one of its hottest Julys on record.

He consulted the discreet but expensive metallic banded watch on his wrist and nodded; he had a few minutes to spare. He couldn't abide poor time-keeping in others and always made a point of never abusing his position of power by keeping others waiting himself. To his mind punctuality was a matter of simple good manners.

As he made his way towards the rear entrance of the large mellow stone building even his well-known critical eye for detail could find no fault in the delightful terraced gardens and wide, well-tended sweeps of green tree-dotted parkland. The pool area, when he reached it, was almost deserted but for a few stalwart—or was it foolish?—tourists sunning themselves in the fiery Majorcan midday sun.

'Did you see who that was?' a female guest hissed excitedly as she clambered wetly out of the pool.

Her sleepy husband opened his eyes reluctantly as wet hands urgently grabbed his shoulder. 'Who…what…?'

'There, it's *Javier Montero!*' she hissed as the tall man in the exquisitely cut suit shook hands in a friendly manner with the elderly gardener before moving away.

'Sure, Javier Montero is on first name terms with all the casual labourers on the island…'

'There's no need to be sarcastic. I tell you, it was him. I mean, there can't be two men who look like him.'

'Don't drool, Jean. And think, woman, what would Javier be doing here?'

'Why wouldn't he be here?' she responded, with a gesture that encompassed the extensive grounds of the thirteenth-century Majorcan manor house with its distinctive Moorish tower. 'He owns the place.'

An army of local craftsmen had returned the once neglected building to its original splendour. Tucked away in the Sierra de Tramuntana the exclusive hotel now provided a hideaway for those people who liked their retreats to combine the most up to date modern conveniences with historic ambience, top-class Mediterranean cuisine and personal attention from helpful staff.

Naturally this combination was very costly, but no more so than the other two hotels the Monteros owned on the island. Each establishment was aimed to appeal to specific clientele. People who wanted the cosmopolitan sophistication of Palma would find everything they could want in the elegant surroundings of the hotel situated right in the middle of the medieval old town; and those who liked a resort that offered them the choice of six top-class restaurants on site, a spa and every sporting facility known to man, with top-class tuition thrown in, would adore the resort hotel on the beautiful undeveloped northern coast of the island.

'Sure, this hotel and God knows how many others around the world, and then there's the airline, the racehorses and the interests in property development. Is there any pie the Monteros don't have a finger in...?' he wondered enviously. 'I really doubt someone like Javier Montero involves himself in the day-to-day running of hotels,' he announced, settling himself back down to sleep.

'It was him.'

'If you say so,' her husband agreed, reapplying sunscreen to his peeling nose—it was too hot to fight.

He had been right on one count; though Javier was known to occasionally subject individual hotels to gruelling spot inspections, it wasn't part of his remit to involve himself in the day-to-day running of individual establishments. Javier's talents lay elsewhere.

Early on in his career he had displayed a remarkable ability for spotting untapped niches in the markets. This talent had been recognised and exploited, but he wasn't just an ideas man; when a project was beset by difficulties, be it labour disputes or legal wranglings, Javier was the person who could be relied upon to get things running.

The information that had brought him hot-foot to the island hardened the naturally severe cast of Javier's staggeringly handsome features as he knocked on the heavy oak-studded door of Serge's office.

Though of average height, due to his massively broad shoulders and deep barrel chest, the swarthy-skinned man behind the desk gave the impression of being much taller.

'Javier!' Serge rose to his feet with a welcoming smile and the two men clasped hands and hugged. 'It's been too long.'

'It has.' Javier responded with the sort of smile that would have shocked rigid those members of the press who had dubbed him Mr Deep Freeze. 'How are little Raul and…Sarah?' Nobody seeing him smile would have guessed that he experienced any difficulty saying this name. 'Where is she? I saw the car…'

'It broke down the last time she was here,' his friend admitted ruefully. 'You can laugh, Javier, but it isn't you that ends up pushing the cursed thing. Other than a stubborn, irrational affection for that old tin can on wheels, Sarah is fine—though your godson is keeping us both up nights.'

'Then I expect you could have done without me asking you to do some discreet digging for me…?'

Serge shook his head. 'Anything I can do, any time— you know this, Javier. I know you don't like me saying this, but if we live to be a hundred there still won't be enough time to pay you back what we owe you.'

'You owe me nothing, Serge.' Abruptly Javier changed the subject. 'About the other thing…' His dark angled eyebrows lifted and his eyes, startling blue in a face that was an even, deep gold, narrowed. 'You're sure about this, Serge?'

Serge sighed and looked grim. 'I'm afraid so. The reports you heard were right.'

'And you know who it is?'

'A waiter working at the resort, a Luis Gonzalez, youngish…about twenty five. He came to work there at the start of the season…'

Javier didn't make a note of the name but Serge knew that he would not forget the name or forgive the guilty party for the crime he had foolishly committed. Javier made a friend in a million but he was an implacable enemy.

'References?' Javier enquired, controlling his impatience; control was one of the things Javier prided himself on.

'Impeccable forgeries.'

'Nobody else is involved, nobody higher…?'

Serge Simeone shook his head.

Javier shrugged and squinted against the midday sun through the window, his expression inscrutable. 'Well, that's something.'

When it had come to his attention that a member of staff in the large resort hotel they owned down on the coast was using his position to deal drugs to guests, Javier, unsure as to how deep the rot was, had not risked involving any of the staff there; instead, he had gone to someone whose integrity he trusted totally.

'You haven't contacted the police yet?'

'You asked me to wait. What are you going to do, Javier?' His friend turned and for a moment Serge experienced a spasm of pity for the culprit. Javier's long, angular, aristocratic face had the texture of cold marble; his deep set eyes were equally chilling. Serge knew that Javier had precious little sympathy with recreational drug use and even less with those who peddled the stuff, after his younger sister had nearly lost her life to addiction.

'We're going to pay Luis a visit.'

Kate Anderson tried not to show her shock as she flicked through the pile of grainy, slightly out-of-focus photos her younger sister had silently handed her after she'd asked, 'Surely they can't be that bad…?' Now she knew they weren't talking a couple of topless shots on the beach which even their conservative parents could have laughed off.

'It could be anyone…?' she croaked, trying desperately to put a positive slant on a very negative situation as she handed them back to her sister, who tore the incriminating images into shreds and let them drop to the floor.

While the negatives were not in their possession, both sisters knew this defiance was just an empty gesture.

'It's not *anyone,* it's *me!* You've got to help me, Kate! You have to do *something,*' Susie added, her expression an accurate reflection of her total faith in her sister's ability to extract her from this present dilemma. After all, she'd been doing it successfully for the past twenty years. 'You can't let mum and dad find out…*I'd die*…'

Kate thought it was much more likely she'd have her generous allowance cut off, but then as far as Susie was concerned that probably amounted to much the same thing!

'That would be…awkward,' Kate admitted thinking of her parents' faces if confronted by semi-nude photos of their younger daughter. She didn't want to think about the consequences if they actually got into the hands of the press. She could think of several tabloids that would love to print compromising shots of a high court judge's daughter.

'What if he sends those photos to *Chris*…? He'll never believe I wasn't sleeping with Luis.'

'*You weren't?*'

Susie's wails got louder. 'See? Even you thought I was. Luis was someone to hang around with and go clubbing, he was fun… You don't believe me,' she accused. 'I can tell…'

'I believe you. Now hush, Susie, I'm thinking…' Kate pleaded as she concentrated on the problem facing them.

The frown line between her feathery brows, which like her lashes were dark in dramatic contrast to the silver-blonde hair colour both sisters had inherited from their mother, deepened as she caught her lower lip between her even white teeth.

Unlike her sister, Kate's features weren't *strictly* symmetrical; her mouth was too wide and full and her aquiline nose had never inspired men to poetry. Her almond-shaped brown eyes, without a doubt her best feature, were unfortunately more often than not concealed behind the round lenses of her wire-framed spectacles.

With or without specs, the first impression people received of Kate Anderson was that she was a young woman with a lively intelligence, sharp wit, and boundless reserves of energy.

'Susie got my looks; Kate's the *sensible* one.' Kate had lost count of the number of times she'd heard her mother explain away her supposed deficiencies to people.

'What she lacks in looks she makes up for in personality,' was her father's kinder assessment.

Kate knew these were essentially accurate assessments, and she hadn't done so badly out of the deal. *Sensible* had given her a lifestyle she enjoyed; but just *occasionally,* especially when she saw the way men reacted when Susie entered a room, she wished that she'd been standing a bit closer to the front of the queue when they'd handed out the sex appeal factor.

A spasm of sulky annoyance passed over Susie's pretty face at this impatient dismissal; her tears in general evoked a more sympathetic response.

Kate dropped down into the wicker chair and pulled her knees up to her chin; her irritation bubbled to the surface. 'What on earth possessed you to get involved with the man in the first place...? You're supposed to be engaged to Chris... Are things all right between you and him, or are you having second thoughts?'

'Don't start on about me being too young to settle down again, Kate!' Susie scowled. 'I'm not like you; I don't want a career and being engaged doesn't mean you can't have any fun,' she announced with a toss of her blonde head.

Kate didn't swallow this hard-nosed attitude for one minute, Susie was wilful but she was a long way from being as callous as she liked to pretend.

'*Fun!* Couldn't you have stuck to beach volley-ball?'

This evoked a watery smile. 'Well, if you had arrived last week, like you were meant to, I wouldn't have been so bored...' Susie stretched one long sun-tanned leg in front of her. The complacent contemplation of the smooth expanse of shapely golden flesh made the sulky line of her lips lift attractively.

Only Susie, Kate decided, could turn this thing around so that her sister had the ultimate responsibility—Susie really was totally impossible, Kate reflected with rueful affection.

'I had to work, you know that.'

'Work?' Susie snorted in disgust. 'It's all you ever think about. No wonder Seb dumped you.' She lifted her head, pushing a strand of long blonde hair from her eyes, and grimaced apologetically. 'Sorry, that was a bitchy thing to say,' she admitted. 'But,' she added swiftly in her own defence, 'this was the holiday from hell, even before Luis turned out to be a low-life, what with Mum and Dad spending every day traipsing around boring churches and things, wanting me to come along.' Her horrified expression was an accurate indicator that these pastimes weren't Susie's idea of pleasure. 'I always said a family holiday at our age was asking for trouble...'

'I thought you decided it wouldn't be so bad when you realised Dad was footing the bill,' Kate couldn't resist observing.

'I just thank God they didn't book that awful place in the mountains you fancied so much. There wasn't anything to do there but watch the grass grow.'

'There also wasn't a Luis.'

'Actually, Katie,' Susie began with an awkward rush, 'the photos…I think he might have spiked my drink when we were by the pool. I mean, I'm not one hundred per cent positive,' she added hurriedly, 'but I know a girl who had her drink spiked…'

Kate's horrified gasp went ignored as her sister, oblivious to the fact she'd said anything to send chills through Kate's blood, continued, 'Oh, she was all right. Fortunately a gang of us arrived as the stuff was kicking in and the guy in question made a quick exit. She collapsed in the loos and we had an awful job getting her back home,' she recalled. 'It's just B—*her* symptoms—' Susie corrected herself with a display of discretion that surprised Kate '—I felt a lot like that. I could hardly get back to my own room, I felt so woozy, and I'd only had a glass of white wine…'

'What a total sleaze!' Kate exclaimed in disgust. 'We should call the police.'

'Get serious, Kate!' Susie responded scornfully. 'I could kick myself. I'm normally really careful about things like that—I never leave my glass on a table, I carry it around with me. Of course, I *never* accept a drink from a man I don't know…'

'Of course,' Kate responded faintly.

As she had listened to Susie casually outlining the list of precautions which were obviously second nature to her, Kate wondered if she was herself extraordinarily trusting or just plain reckless, because even though she'd heard of such things happening since the advent of the so-called date rape drugs, she had never dreamt of taking any of these measures… But then she had never dated a stranger; her boyfriends such as they were had always been friends of friends or work colleagues.

'What really gets me, is that he didn't even *try* and touch me… It was Dad's money he was interested in all along, not me!'

'Well thank God for that!'

'I just feel such a fool. I was wondering how I was going to let him down lightly; I thought he was potty about me. God, Katie!' she wailed. 'What am I going to do…?'

Placing a comforting arm around the younger girl's shaking shoulders, Kate hugged her tight. She crossed her fingers. 'Don't worry, Suse, it'll be all right.' *I hope!*

'Then you'll lend me the money to pay him off…?' Susie lifted her tear stained face eagerly.

'We're not giving him a penny,' Kate responded, her tone outraged at the idea of giving into a blackmailer. 'I'll get the photos and the negatives.'

'But how?'

'That,' admitted Kate frankly, 'I haven't worked out yet.'

'Listen, Kate, I don't think this is such a good idea. I mean, Luis isn't going to hand them over, is he? And once or twice I've seen him talking with some shifty-looking types. Actually, I think he could be quite mean himself…' She gave a shamefaced little grin. 'I suppose, if I'm honest, that was half the attraction…the danger thing,' she sniffed. 'You know what I mean…' She looked at her elder sister who pushed her specs up the bridge of her nose. 'I don't suppose you do. I know you think I'm a selfish little cow but even I might lose an hour or two's sleep if you got hurt because of me.'

Kate pulled a tissue from the pocket of her shorts and dabbed her sister's pink nose. 'Don't fret. I've no intention of getting hurt, Suse.'

Kate had waited an hour in the darkness watching the staff bungalow until she was satisfied there was nobody home. The wait had taken its toll, by the time she tentatively tried the door she felt physically sick with nerves and her heart was pounding so loud, its frantic, echoey thud cut out all other sounds. She couldn't recall ever feeling this scared, not even the first time she'd made her court appearance as a newly qualified barrister.

She could hardly believe her luck when the door opened at the first try. Relieved she wouldn't have to put her admittedly hazy knowledge of lock picking—second hand, naturally—to the test, Kate slid the credit card she'd brought for the purpose into the back pocket of her dark jeans and adjusted the dark hood on her head so that it covered all her pale hair.

Shining her torch around the darkened room, she picked her way stealthily through the discarded garments littering the carpet. Her skin crawled and she stifled a scream as her foot got entangled in a shirt. This whole enterprise was making her feel grubby. After this is over I'll need a stiff drink and a bath, not necessarily in that order she thought as she carefully balanced the torch on top of the chest of drawers.

Her hands were shaking so much, it took her two goes to slide the top drawer open. Concentrate, Kate she told herself, taking a deep fortifying breath. It's my lucky day she decided as her fingers closed around an envelope—the shape of which felt very promising...

Her newly fortified wits fled gibbering in panic as the room was suddenly flooded with strong light from a powerful flashlight that dwarfed her own feeble beam. Before she even had a chance to turn around, a pair of strong arms snaked around her, pinning one arm to her chest as, arched backwards by the tight embrace, her feet were lifted off the ground.

Her rudimentary Spanish could not cope with the staccato burst of furious-sounding words which hissed like bullets in her ear. With Susie's warnings about this blackmailer and his shady friends ringing in her ears, she began to struggle wildly. With her free arm she flailed backwards, trying to inflict as much damage as possible, enough at least to make her captor loosen his grip. A chair and several sundry items, including her glasses, were casualties of her frenzied efforts to free herself.

Only this captor wasn't letting her go, not even when she brought her trainer-shod heel—stilettos would have produced much more satisfactory results—down viciously onto his instep, the way they'd taught her in self-defence class. She took small comfort from the fact it must have hurt like hell because he cursed—at least it sounded like a curse.

Kate wasn't a short woman and, though slim, she wasn't delicate—she kept herself fit, she ran and enjoyed playing sports—but it soon became clear to her that she was vastly outclassed. It was obvious that restraining her was not overly exerting her captor, who wasn't even breathing heavily. A pragmatist, she quickly accepted she couldn't fight her way out of this situation—that left talking her way out, and she was good at that…

'Please…let me go!' she panted, forcing her body to go limp.

'English?'

The startled exclamation across the room was the first indication to her that she wasn't only outclassed but outnumbered too.

'You're English?' The low, cultured voice close to her ear had only the faintest husky tinge of an attractive accent.

This must be one of the waiter's sinister friends, she reasoned, recalling Susie's comments on Luis's charming broken English—unless that too had been part of his scam.

'Of course I'm English!' she exclaimed at her most haughty.

'A woman…?' The voice from across the room exclaimed.

'I had noticed,' her captor replied drily before switching to rapid Spanish.

Probably issuing instructions about where to dispose of my body, Kate thought, as she struggled in vain to catch the gist of what was being said. Her mind was working furiously. How long will it be before anyone misses me...? Not until morning at the earliest, she realised with dismay.

She'd excused herself early from dinner with her parents, pleading a headache, and if Susie had carried on drinking wine at the rate she had been when Kate had left she would now either be dead to the world or dancing the night away in the nearest night-club.

'I'm going to put you down now. Do not try to escape.'

Kate nodded her head compliantly whilst privately vowing to do just the opposite should the opportunity arise.

Released from the iron grip and with her feet back on the ground, Kate's knees displayed the consistency of cotton wool. Fortunately her spirit was more resilient. Chin up—not too much: she didn't want to come across as bolshy, more an innocent victim of circumstance—she turned to face her aggressors.

'Will you take that thing out of my eyes?' she appealed, lifting a hand to shield her eyes from the glare of the torch.

After a moment someone responded to her request.

She could now see, though the loss of her specs meant the one standing some way away was nothing but a blurred outline suggestive of threatening bulk. The one who had held her was another matter! He was close enough for her to see quite well. Like herself, he was clad from head to toe in black. There the similarity ended!

The hard, lean, muscle-packed torso Kate already knew about from her struggles; the rest of the package reduced her to a stunned silence. She blinked several times as she assimilated the attributes of her assailant, who ironically turned out to be the most physically perfect specimen of manhood she'd ever come across. These numerous attributes included ridiculously broad shoulders, snaky slim hips and long legs, and then there was his face…!

And what a face! God I'm thinking in superlatives, some objective corner of her mind observed as she drank in the details of his long, arrestingly attractive, angular features. His was a starkly uncompromising face—a high intelligent forehead, an almost hawkish nose reminiscent of the strong Moorish inheritance she'd seen reflected in many parts of Spain, his beautifully sculpted slashing cheekbones stretched his even golden-toned skin taut and his mouth was an intriguing combination of control and passion. The jutting angles and sculpted planes married sweetly, giving their owner a countenance that could never be overlooked in a crowd, but combined with his incongruously blue eyes, fringed with extravagant lush lashes and slanted ebony brows, the exceptional became the extraordinary.

The deep-set, startling blue eyes narrowed as he subjected her to a scrutiny just as thorough as her own of him—he didn't appear overly impressed by what he saw. 'Now, *señorita*, where is Gonzalez?' he demanded impatiently.

CHAPTER TWO

MUTELY Kate shook her head.

He subjected her to another glare of biting derision before abruptly firing a quick sentence in Spanish at his companion who immediately extinguished the light.

For a moment there was total inky darkness. Kate, her brain working frantically, began to speculate on her chances of getting to the door before she was caught. It had to be evens or better? What did she have to lose? Quite a lot, actually, came the instant reply, and besides you haven't got the photos yet.

'*Don't even think about it.*'

She jumped as the wry voice emerged from the inky blackness, slicing through her frantic thoughts of escape.

The owner's powerful profile that matched the dark dangerous drawl was revealed as the second man pulled back the curtain, allowing the moonlight to filter into the room.

Kate blinked, dazzled, as the flashlight once more swept across her face; it moved past her and she saw the second man shake his head.

'Are you expecting him tonight?' The tall one, who had boss written all over him, recommended his interrogation.

'I've never met Gonzalez,' she rebutted honestly.

Kate suspected she might be in the middle of a falling out between villains; she didn't want to accidentally reveal anything that might make her position even more precarious.

Under the circumstances, playing dumb might not be so hard, she decided bitterly, because only someone spectacularly stupid would have blundered in here like this! They must, she reasoned—*now* I can reason!—have been lying in wait.

Her guileless response evoked no softening in the magnificently moody face of her sinister interrogator.

'You just wandered in here by accident…?' His eyes skimmed the outfit she'd chosen for her first foray into breaking and entering. 'Dressed like that?' A derisive snort emerged from between those fascinating lips—*cruel* lips, she thought, unable to control the fearful little shudder that chased along her spine.

'You're one to talk,' she retorted, peering myopically from one man to the other; both their muscular bodies were sheathed in close-fitting black outfits. We must look like a convention of cat burglars; her full lips twitched at the mental image of a social gathering of black-clad thieves.

'You find something funny about this?' he grated incredulously.

The second man had faded into the shadows, apparently content to let his partner in crime do all the talking—perhaps he was the muscle. Not that this guy looked like he needed any help in that area, she mused, as her eyes slid over his impressive torso—not an ounce of spare flesh anywhere that she could see. In fact, in that close-fitting top, if she squinted she could just about make out the slabs of individual muscle across… *Stop!* The warning voice inside her head shrieked.

Kate took a deep breath and pushed her fear and lustful speculation aside as she tried to view the situation objectively—or at least without gibbering fearfully or drooling lustfully. If she was going to get out of this, *he* was the one she had to talk round, she decided, weighing up her opposition objectively. What she saw was not wildly encouraging. She'd seen rock faces with more give than that chiselled jawline.

'Oh, yes, I'm just *wild* about being jumped on in the dark by some stupid big thug,' she was frustrated into com-

menting bitterly. She prodded her aching ribs tentatively.
'I'll probably be black and blue tomorrow, which isn't a
good look in a bikini...' she grumbled, even though she
favoured one-piece bathing suits. Talking, even if she was
talking rubbish, gave her time to think... At least, that was
the theory...

'If I'm such a vicious thug of limited intelligence,
shouldn't you be treating me with a little more respect...?'

The man had a point and, as for the intelligence part, if
those alert eyes were any indication at all he had a brain
like a steel trap.

'Is that a threat?'

'If I threaten you, you'll know about it.'

'I see not a threat, just a boast.' With dismay, she saw a
flicker of interest enter those laser-like eyes—she didn't
want his interest. Her release from this depended on him
considering her harmless and an air of stupidity wouldn't
do her case any harm either. Despite this conviction, she
couldn't stop herself adding, 'I'm normally prepared to give
anyone the benefit of the doubt, but in this instance I don't
think there's any *if* about it. You are a vicious thug and
yes, I probably should shut up, but when I'm nervous I
babble...always have done...'

'I don't think you're nervous,' he cut in smoothly. 'I
think that under that wide-eyed candour you're as hard as
nails. Did you arrange to meet Gonzalez here? Or did he
perhaps ask you to pick something up for him? Does he
know we're on to him? Well?'

'It won't do you any good to bully me.' She saw a flicker
of amazement chase across his strong-boned features and
wondered if she was being daring or just plain stupid to
antagonise him. The truth was, she couldn't help herself;
something about this man made her want to score points...

'I am not a bully!' he refuted in an irritated steely drawl.

She smiled in polite disbelief and heard what might have

been his even white teeth grinding. 'And it won't do you any good,' she elaborated. 'Because I've not the faintest idea what you're talking about.' She shook her head so emphatically that the hood of her sweat top slipped off her head.

One dark brow rose as her silver-blonde tresses tumbled free from the loose knot she'd hastily confined them in on her head. Her stomach lurched as, with studied insolence, those electric-blue eyes moved over her body pausing overly long in significant areas.

Kate's first instinct was to cover herself with her hands. She almost immediately saw how ludicrous and demeaning her response to the earthy sexual appraisal was, and let her hands fall away; in doing so she saw the strands of dark hair caught in her fist.

Unobtrusively she wriggled her fingers to dislodge them; it didn't seem wise to remind someone with such violent inclinations of the no doubt painful moment when her fingers had become blindly entangled in his hair—lush, silky hair, she recalled. Her fingertips tingled uncomfortably as her brain replayed the sensation. With a head of hair like that, she thought practically, he wasn't going to miss the little bit she had ripped out.

'Or maybe you knew he wasn't here... Maybe this is a bit of private enterprise...? You were taking advantage of his absence to help yourself?' He fired the fresh volley of questions at her like bullets without removing his unnerving gaze from her face for even a second. 'What was she about to take out of the drawer, Serge?'

It was spooky. This man it seemed didn't feel the need to blink—but then he probably had iced water running through his veins, not blood, she thought, rubbing her arms where a rash of goosebumps had broken out.

'It's true I didn't come here by accident exactly,' Kate admitted with discomfort as the silent second man, moving with surprising speed for one so large, headed towards the chest of drawers.

Apprehension made Kate's pulse rate soar, an acceptable thing to happen to the most cool-headed of individuals, given the circumstances; the problem was, Kate knew it was only part of the story—there was in fact a much more significant factor. The main reason for the state of near-collapse of her nervous system was—*that man!* She glared angrily up at the stranger's dark saturnine face and her insides tightened another painful notch.

The man projected raw sexuality like a force field; she'd never come across anything like it! However, now was no time to analyse her curiously strong reaction to her cold-eyed interrogator; she needed to be clear headed and focused.

Being clear-headed wasn't as easy as it sounded when you couldn't rid yourself of a nasty, nagging suspicion. What if Susie wasn't the only Anderson who was attracted by danger…? Especially when it came so spectacularly packaged. Oh, God, I'm so shallow! In the future she definitely wouldn't be making so free with her superior sniffs and pitying looks, Kate decided, swallowing a large dose of humility.

'I came here to retrieve something, but it doesn't belong to this Mr Gonzalez. It's…mine.' She kept her voice cool enough but she couldn't stop her eyes darting nervously in the direction of the bulky figure who was sifting through the contents of the drawer, which were now scattered on the ground.

A combination of nerves and the heat in the room made Kate's thin sweatshirt cling damply to her back; sweat pooled uncomfortably in the hollow between her breasts. Conscious of the constant presence of those piercing blue eyes drilling into her skull, she licked her lips nervously.

She'd studied enough guilty people to know she was displaying all the classic signs of guilt herself.

'She was holding this, I think, Javier.'

Kate couldn't stop herself from lunging wildly forwards for the parcel of photographs as they passed between the two men. 'They're mine!' she yelled.

For several stubborn seconds she resisted the compulsion of fingers like iron which closed mercilessly around her wrist before her stiffly clenched fingers unfurled. Tears of pain and frustration standing out in her eyes, she glared resentfully up at her persecutor.

'You've no right...' Her voice faded away as the one she now knew was called Javier slid one long finger under the sealed opening of the package. Paralysed by horror, she watched as he withdrew one glossy print and held it up.

Kate's face flamed as his clinical glance moved from the photo in his hand to her and back again before he slid it back in. He pulled out a strip of negatives and held it up to the light. His nostrils flared and his lips quivered faintly in an attitude of fastidious distaste as he briefly viewed the images revealed.

The other man shot him a question in Spanish which he replied to in the same language—the reply made the other man laugh in surprise. Kate's hands balled into fists as she gritted her teeth; every natural feeling in her rebelled at the idea of these two sniggering at her Susie's expense.

'Do you do this sort of thing for a living, or is it just a hobby?'

He thinks they're pictures of me! Kate's jaw dropped. In other circumstances she might have felt flattered to have her body confused with that of her lovely younger sister, but on this occasion it just made her flip. Where moments before she had felt embarrassed and defensively protective of Susie, now she experienced a flash of blazingly hot rage.

If her adversary hadn't possessed startlingly swift reactions, her closed-fisted blow would have made contact with his lean cheek. Kate, who had never felt the need to resort to anything as crude as brute force in her life experienced a moment of confusion and shock at her actions before the overpowering need to escape overwhelmed her.

'Let me go!' she shrieked, landing a kick on his shins before she subsided her eyes flashing, her breath coming in short gasps. Her nostrils quivered; underneath the light expensive male fragrance he wore she could smell the clean-washed, spicy, masculine scent that she'd noticed before she'd even laid eyes on him—it had bothered her then, and it bothered her more now.

'Now you show your true colours,' came the disdainful observation. 'Cool down, little cat. I have no interest in your sleazy snaps; you can have them...'

Kate felt so pathetically relieved by this contemptuous information that she could have wept. Trying to retain a semblance of dignity, still panting from her exertions, she looked pointedly at his dark fingers still encircling her wrist and did her best to ignore the languid contempt in his tone. She couldn't afford to lose her temper; he had the photos and for Susie's sake she had to get them, even if this involved a bit of humiliation.

With an unpleasant, sneery sort of smile that made Kate's fingers itch to remove it from his smug face, he released her hand and mockingly inclined his glossy head. '...When I have the information I require,' he completed the white crocodile smile fading completely.

Kate's shoulders slumped as her eyes stayed trained on the photos held tantalisingly out of reach. She was fast coming to the conclusion he was playing cat and mouse games with her and, the awful part was, there wasn't a thing she could do about it.

'I don't know anything.' She sighed wearily as she rubbed her tender wrist; the imprint of those strong brown fingers seemed to be branded into her flesh.

'Cut the innocent act. You obviously know him, unless you send pornographic pictures of yourself to total strangers...?' he sneered.

Pink spots of outrage appeared on her smooth cheeks. 'They are not pornographic, they're…they're *tasteful,*' she finished, unable to repress a weak grimace at the memory of the photos.

'Sure they're art,' he drawled insultingly. 'What's the connection? Is he your lover, or your supplier?'

'Supplier?' she exclaimed. Her eyes widened as her frown of incomprehension lifted. *'Drugs!'* Oh, God, what have I walked into? Had Luis Gonzalez tried to muscle in on the big boys? Were these men here to teach him a lesson, or worse…? 'This is a m-misunderstanding,' she stuttered. 'I know nothing about any drugs.'

'Of course you don't.'

Her eyes filled with tears of sheer frustration. She blinked hard to stop them spilling over. If she could weep like Susie—it was one of life's mysteries how Susie cried so picturesquely—tears might get her somewhere, but she couldn't see this man being touched by her own blotchy face and runny nose.

'Why won't you believe me? Do I look like a drug addict or something?'

'And what do they look like?' If he'd been so damned good at spotting the signs, Javier reflected bitterly, his sister would have been spared those agonising months of rehabilitation.

'You should know. It's your business, not mine.'

He went rigid. Not a muscle in his face moved, but his eyes blazed like twin points of fury. 'Women like you are incomprehensible! Why do you protect him?' he demanded. 'Is it fear, or some misplaced sense of loyalty? A man like that will pull you down to his level, and when you get there he'll leave you…'

Without any warning he grabbed her arm and, swiftly rolling up the sleeve of her top, ran one long finger softly over the blue-veined inner aspect of her left wrist and forearm. Under the light his accessory helpfully directed over the area, his keen eyes searched her fair blemishless skin for tell-tale marks.

Kate shivered helplessly as tingling arrows of electricity shot up her arm. Instinctively she started to pull back and then stopped as a strange heavy lethargy stole over her. Her leaden-lidded eyes were riveted on the image of his dark fingers on her skin; heat travelled like a flash-flood, bathing her entire body; the distant buzzing in her head got closer.

She only started breathing again when he released her.

'Satisfied now?' With dignity she rolled down her sleeve.

'Not quite.'

Her stomach muscles clenched as she saw his intention. Her angry dark eyes clashed with his emotionless gaze for several seconds before she conceded defeat.

'Let me,' she said sarcastically as she turned back the sleeve that covered her right arm. Chin lifted defiantly, she thrust out her arm in front of him.

She waited for him to look away, embarrassed, shocked or maybe repelled—she'd seen all the reactions which, to her mind, were wildly out of proportion to the small puckered area of skin, pinker than the rest of her skin, that lay along the inside of her arm, just above her elbow joint—there was another, smaller and less prominent area on her shoulderblade which the plastic surgery had not quite been able to conceal.

It was amazing how such a small blemish could throw some people and make them look at you differently. Kate had decided a long time ago that other people's squeamishness was their problem, not hers, and she didn't go out of her way to conceal or reveal the childhood scars she still bore from a domestic accident.

This man wasn't thrown. Neither did he fall into the category of those who politely pretended not to notice the marks. Seb had been one of those—Seb who, despite his protests that it really didn't matter to him, had never been able to bring himself to touch the scarred area.

This man had no such qualms. He took the arm she defiantly offered between his big hands and turned it slightly sideways, rubbing his thumb lightly over the shiny scar tissue as he did so. Kate shivered and the blue eyes lifted momentarily.

'A burn?' There was not a shred of pity in his expression and over the years Kate had become something of an expert at detecting it.

She cleared her throat, it felt raw and achey. 'Are you always this morbidly curious…?'

'You are not comfortable discussing it?'

Not just mad, bad and indisputably dangerous, he had to turn out to be into amateur psychology—this just got better and better! 'Not with homicidal maniacs.'

'Do you know many homicidal maniacs?'

Kate shook her head. 'Most murders are domestic,' she announced authoritatively. 'If you've seen enough…do you mind…?' she added, with a cool nod to her arm. It was hard to project cool when this man's touch made her shiver.

He straightened up and their eyes met again. Kate had the impression he saw through her bravado, saw right through to the insecure teenager she'd once been, still learning to cope with the occasional stare or rude comment. Disliking the feeling of vulnerability, she shook her head to dispel the scary illusion as she pulled the fabric back down over her arm.

'I hope,' he remonstrated severely, touching the stretchy cotton fabric of her top, 'you do not cover yourself all the time.'

This whole situation, she decided, was getting distinctly surreal. She was getting personal advice from someone who waited in dark rooms for blackmailing drug-dealers. Perhaps working with the criminals had given her a unique rapport with the fraternity; if her mother was to be believed, it had given her a twisted and cynical outlook on life.

'Only when I'm doing a spot of breaking and entering.'

She bit her lip. Irony was a luxury a person in her position could not afford. Then, emboldened by the unexpected gleam of amusement in his eyes, she nodded towards the photos. 'Listen,' she continued in her most persuasive tone—there was no point dismissing out of hand the slim possibility that he was human, after all. 'I honestly don't know your friend, so why don't I just leave and forget I ever saw you?'

'*Friend? Por Dios…!*'

Kate backed away from the lash of contemptuous fury in his voice and carried on backing nervously until the sound of the heavy-set second thug clearing his throat significantly brought her to an abrupt halt. She looked over her shoulder and discovered he was positioned, arms folded across his massive chest, in front of the only exit.

'I tell you, I don't know him. I'm just a guest here. I only arrived today…'

As she'd appealed to his partner, the second man sauntered up to join him—Kate had almost forgotten his silent presence. She turned her head as the flashlight he carried shone momentarily in her eyes. 'If we let her go, she could warn him we're on to him.'

The sinister significance of this observation was not lost on Kate, who paled with alarm. '*If,*' she exclaimed shrilly. 'What do you mean, if? You lay a finger or try and stop me leaving and I'll make so much noise…'

The one in command winced at her shrill tone. 'Make any more noise than you already are and a concerned guest or member of staff might call the police.'

The best news she'd heard all day—and a long, *long* day it had been. Had it only been this morning she'd boarded the flight to Palma…? Somehow this wasn't quite the Sangria and sunset sort of end to the day she'd anticipated.

'Let's cut out the middle man,' she suggested tartly, reaching for the phone and holding it out to him. Her scars might not have fazed him but Kate could tell her response had taken him aback, and maybe he was right. Maybe she was acting foolishly—somehow, though, she didn't think tears and pleas were going to get her very far.

'And I would naturally feel obligated to hand over these,' he tauntingly wafted the pack of photos in front of her nose.

'And they'd believe your story? I think I might have a little more credibility with the police than you,' she countered calling his bluff.

For some reason, this claim caused his companion to laugh, though he did sober up fast enough when he was on the receiving end of a silencing glare.

'You think so?'

He wasn't to her mind displaying the sort of dismay a shady character like him ought to when threatened with the forces of law. Perhaps he hid his illicit dealings behind a legitimate front, she speculated uneasily.

'I'm a very respectable person.'

'Now, I might be swayed by the throbbing note of conviction and the big brown eyes…but the police, they generally like more concrete proof…'

'You want proof…right.' With a triumphant smile of pure relief she remembered the card in her pocket. 'That's me, K. M. Anderson.' She shoved her credit card under his nose. 'I'm sharing one of the bungalows with my—with a friend…' No need, she decided, to involve Susie.

'You could have stolen it,' he replied glancing without interest at her gold card. 'In fact, under the circumstances, I'd say that's highly likely.'

Kate's chest swelled with indignation, a fact that didn't escape her tormentor's notice. Kate's eyes began to sparkle angrily as his eyes dropped with unabashed interest on the heaving contours. To her horror, she felt her nipples harden and peak.

Lecherous creep, she thought, her anger intensified by the treacherous reactions of her body and the accelerated rate of her heartbeat.

'One of the things I hate most in this world is men who can't keep their eyes on a woman's face when they're talking to her!' she announced with scornful defiance.

That refocused his attention all right; the astonished blue gaze instantly zoomed in on her face.

The startled gasp, followed by a low chuckle, didn't come from the man whose enigmatic scrutiny was making her wish like mad she'd kept quiet on the subject, but from his partner.

'As I was saying,' she began doggedly, 'I didn't steal the card. It's mine. I brought it along in case the door was...' She stopped abruptly, her eyes growing round in dismay as she bit back the incriminating explanation.

'Locked...?' The fascinating network of fine lines around his cerulean eyes deepened.

Kate felt her guilty blush deepen.

'What a resourceful woman you are.... You still haven't told me what you're doing here.'

'Why should I? You haven't told me why you're here and I'm pretty sure it's not by invitation,' she murmured stroppily.

'Hush!' he admonished, cutting her off with abrupt urgency before turning to his companion. 'Serge, did you hear that?'

The hot flare of anticipation Kate glimpsed in his blue eyes suggested to her that she was dealing with an adrenaline junkie, the type who got high on danger, she speculated. The sort that took risks and got a kick out of doing so. She'd often noted these two qualities, allied with a callous disregard for the law, in some of her clients—men who, had they channelled their talents into less anti-social endeavours, would probably have made very successful businessmen, or even for that matter lawyers like herself.

The other man nodded and replied softly. 'It could be Gonzalez?'

The light was suddenly doused and Kate's hopeful ears

were rewarded by the sound of footsteps on the paved area outside the window. She didn't care who it was, it was the chance she'd been waiting for. She opened her mouth to cry for help.

Before she had a chance to raise the alarm, a large hand clamped down hard over her parted lips whilst another twisted her arm behind her back. 'You want to warn your lover?' a cold, hateful voice rasped mockingly in her ear, Kate tried to turn her head, hating his contempt, hating the sensation of his warm breath on her neck, and fearing the confusing ripples of sensation it created. 'I don't think so…'

Biting his hand as hard as she could was not the most subtle response, but Kate was desperate by this point.

He didn't cry out, even though she felt the salty tang of blood on her tongue, but his grip did slacken—only slightly, but it was the moment Kate had been tensely waiting for. It was enough to allow her to break free. With a determined, sinuous wriggle, she twisted away from him and even before she was upright began to run. Head down, she hit the floor, running like a sprinter ducking desperately for the winning line.

CHAPTER THREE

KATE opened her eyes and moaned. She looked around groggily. This was new—waking up in a strange bed, in a strange bedroom. Not all new experiences were good ones and actually this was one she could well have lived without!

She couldn't have amnesia. She knew her name; she could even recite her pin number and other personal details. She just didn't recall the events that had culminated in her being in this bed—maybe this was an occurrence some girls could take in their stride, but not her. Don't panic, Kate, she told herself, there has to be a perfectly simple explanation for this.

The problem was, try as she might, she couldn't come up with it. She attacked the problem with her usual vigour and all she got for her troubles was a brain ache.

The last thing she remembered was getting on the flight for Palma; her memories of that were perfectly clear. She'd ended up holding a baby all the way for the harassed young mother travelling alone with two active toddlers and a fretful six-month-old. The mother had been grateful; the baby had expressed his gratitude by throwing up all over her cream linen designer suit.

The unthinkable suddenly occurred to her. What if she wasn't alone in the strange bed? Holding her breath, she reached behind her, a relieved sigh escaped her lips as the search came up empty.

Javier entered the room just as she was blindly patting the pillow, her eyes screwed tightly shut. He heard her hoarse sigh from the other side of the room. A spasm of amusement lightened the severity of his lean, dark features as he approached, a nightdress folded over one arm.

It wasn't too hard to interpret his guest's actions. Ms K. M. Anderson—it hadn't taken long to discover that they did indeed have a K. M. Anderson staying—was wondering if she'd woken up beside a stranger. From her reactions, it seemed safe to assume this wasn't an everyday occurrence for her.

Javier found himself idly wondering what her response would have been if her hand had encountered his own body instead of the pillow lying there beside her. For a brief moment he imagined her turning, arms outstretched, a smile of invitation on those full sexy lips. Reality intervened; it was much more likely, considering her reckless streak, she'd have picked up the nearest heavy blunt object and knocked him senseless with it. All the same, even his remarkable will power could not totally banish the lingering image of warm, welcoming arms.

Frowning, Kate rolled onto her back. The large fans swooshing silently overhead seemed in keeping with the tasteful and expensive Colonial-style furnishings in the room around her. Her parents' beachfront bungalow had similar furnishing, though it wasn't nearly as spacious.

Of course! She was on holiday. She was in bed at the hotel in the room she shared with Susie... Her relieved expression faded—this theory only worked to a point. This lavishly appointed space wasn't their much more modest bedroom with its twin beds, rattan furniture and a nice view of one of the pools from the dinky veranda.

'My head hurts,' she complained out loud.

'I'm not surprised.'

'You!' Kate shrieked in loathing.

She shot bolt upright, bristling with antipathy. The mystery of her brain blanking out the last few hours was a mystery no longer; it had merely been a protective reflex. Protecting her from the worst day of her life.

'How did I get here?' Not under her own steam, that much she knew, and where was 'here'? 'Kidnapping is a very serious offence.' It was in England, and she had no reason to believe the Spanish treated this offence any differently.

One slanted brow rose politely. 'So I believe.'

It was frustratingly apparent her stern warning hadn't had any effect on his bone-deep air of assurance—other than to infuse it with a slight edge of infuriating, indulgent amusement—but then why would it…? She was talking to a hardened, desperate criminal. There was every likelihood he had probably done a lot worse than kidnapping! Perhaps he still thought she was some junkie who nobody would miss?

'And there are people who will miss me…*lots* of people…' She broke off abruptly clutching her head as an arrow of agony shot through her temple.

Through a miasma of pain, Kate felt the mattress give as he came to sit on the edge; her nose quivered as she encountered the attractive male fragrance emanating from his warm body—any closer and she might feel the warmth too. Kate tensed at the thought. This was getting way too intimate for her liking! With a muffled cry of protest that hurt her head, she tried to shuffle blindly away, but a firm hand on her elbow prevented her.

'I won't hurt you.' Kate was mad with herself for instinctively believing him, despite all the evidence to the contrary. 'You should lie down; you took quite a knock.'

'You should know, you probably delivered it,' she retorted through gritted teeth.

'Actually you ran full pelt into the wardrobe—solid mahogany. Renewable sources of course; the owners have a very green policy…'

This information did actually correspond with Kate's

own hazy recollection of the incident. 'You make it sound as if I did it on purpose,' she muttered truculently. 'Actually, I had my eyes closed.' Like now.

Her blue-veined eyelids flickered as she felt the pad of one fingertip brush aside a strand of hair from her forehead. Her mind supplied a vivid lifelike image—possibly aided by the fact she could still smell his elusive male scent—to go with the action. The image of long, sensitive, tapering fingers, very dark in dramatic contrast to her fair creamy skin, lingered in her mind as her stomach muscles began to quiver uncomfortably.

Keeping her eyes closed, she told herself, had nothing to do with being afraid of seeing his raw sex appeal up close. The light hurt her eyes—that was all.

'From the look of your spectacle lenses, it wouldn't have made much difference if you'd had them open,' he murmured, his deep voice laced with disparaging amusement. 'Does the light hurt your eyes?'

'A little.' Kate was willing to ignore this insulting slur on her eyesight. He had her glasses—she needed them, and much as it went against the grain it was time for a bit of pleading. 'You've got my glasses? Give them to me.' She opened her eyes. '*Please,*' she added gruffly. 'Being without them is like…like being naked.' It was hard enough to explain the vulnerability of being short-sighted to anyone not similarly afflicted, but to someone as genetically perfect as this man it was probably a waste of breath.

His perfection was hard to miss this close too. She didn't need her specs to assimilate the dark, brooding magnificence of his strong-boned features—looking at them alarmingly intensified the dizziness she was experiencing.

'I'm afraid I stepped on them in the dark.'

'You did it deliberately!' she heard herself wail childishly.

'They say your other senses compensate…'

Kate watched with total fascination as his long fingers made a stroking sensation a hair's breath away from the pale skin of her forearm. As if those well manicured fingertips were electrified, the fine hairs on her skin became erect.

Was this the unnatural affinity she'd heard abductees developed with their kidnappers? she wondered hazily as her insides dissolved in the flood of scalding liquid heat which cascaded through her body. Like hell it is, Kate! Face facts! This is lust, sexual attraction—at least, on my side—plain and simple. His motivation for playing cat and mouse games were less immediately obvious.

'...when one sense is compromised,' the insidiously sexy drawl continued. 'In my experience, closing my eyes often enhances and heightens tactile sensations...'

Her shameless brain immediately provided several steamy images of situations where he might feel obliged to close his eyes. The situations revealed in those fragmented images uniformly necessitated him being naked, his golden skin gleaming beneath a layer of sweat. The hoarse groan of pleasure she imagined being ripped from his throat was so realistic that a swiftly subdued whimper emerged from her own throat—this was getting out of hand.

So the man was incredibly good-looking, sinfully sexy and packed more masculinity into his little finger than most men did in their entire bodies... That was no excuse to lose the plot, Kate told herself sternly.

'This might help that naked feeling you were talking about.'

Kate looked blankly from his enigmatic face to the creamy cotton scoop-necked nightdress he handed her. Her brain made the link between his words and the garment and she bit her lip. She wasn't—was she?

She hardly dared, but she forced herself to look downwards at her own body—it could have been worse, but not much. Her skin looked dramatically pale against the black of the simple bra she wore; she couldn't see them but she knew her matching pants would afford an equally stark contrast.

'You took my clothes off!' she choked, her voice shaking with outrage and suspicion. Was that all he'd done...?

'I did,' he confirmed, coolly unapologetic. 'It seemed the most sensible thing to do under the circumstances. You were burning up.'

If she hadn't been, she was now! With a fraught squawk of dismay, she belatedly slid beneath the duvet, leaving only her face and tousled ash-blonde hair peeking out.

One dark brow rose expressively. 'There is really no need for a display of false modesty; women on the beach wear less than you are.' One corner of his mouth lifted as a devilish gleam appeared in his eyes. 'Considerably less, actually,' he added drily. 'Or are you afraid you'll inflame my lust? Don't...I have strong control.'

In other words, he wasn't that desperate!

His languid drawl sent an extra-sharp stab of pain through Kate's pounding skull. Though she never normally envied Susie her looks, at that moment she wouldn't have minded having the equipment to make this man eat his contemptuous words.

'Oh, yes, you struck me right off as someone *oozing* strong moral fibre,' she sneered, oozing hostility. 'And as for women on the beach, *they* haven't been interfered with by a raving lunatic.'

'Do you always have such lurid fantasies?'

Kate's cheeks flamed. With one quirk of an eyebrow he'd managed to give the distinct impression he wouldn't touch her with a ten foot barge pole. 'None involving you!'

An honest girl, Kate knew she would in the future. It was inevitable; he was the sort of male that made the female unconscious run riot. She just hoped her fantasies

would wait until she was safe in the bosom of her family—
she refused to allow herself to contemplate *if.* She was going to get away from this man.

Javier saw her wince. 'You really should not shout or
get agitated,' he remonstrated.

'Advice from you I can do without.'

He gave a shrug. 'I removed your clothes because you
were dressed inappropriately for the weather conditions.
Though ideally for a spot of larceny,' he added slyly.

'Are you calling me a thief?' she gritted.

'If the cap fits…?'

'Takes one to know one…' she countered childishly.

'Takes a thief to catch a thief,' he riposted without a
pause.

'Gosh, your colloquial English is really very good.' I
can't believe I just said that…! I've been knocked unconscious, kidnapped, I'm lying as good as naked in a strange
bed in the company of an indisputably dangerous man who
could do anything at any moment and all I can do is admire
his grammar…!

His heavy lids drooped hiding the expression in his deep
set eyes momentarily from Kate. 'The British, they're just
priceless.'

'Pardon?'

Those lush dark lashes lifted off his cheekbones revealing cynical blue. 'Shades of the empire; you refuse to learn
another language and delight in commenting on foreigners'
funny accents.'

Kate, who was mortified by this interpretation of her unthinking observation, couldn't help but observe that his
deep velvety drawl could be classified as many things, including dangerously seductive, but *funny* wasn't one of
them!

'I didn't mean it like that!' she exclaimed, horrified to
have him lump her together with an unpleasant, ignorant

minority she had nothing whatever in common with. 'Anyhow, it's an absurd generalisation, and I was *not* being patronising.' Why am I making such a fuss? she wondered eyeing the good-looking cause of her discomfort resentfully. His good opinion is not something I'm going to lie awake at nights thinking about—now his mouth, that was another matter, her wilful thoughts added naughtily.

'You look feverish.'

Kate stiffened as a cool hand touched her perspiring forehead—she could hardly explain the likely reason for her sweaty state. The hand lifted and she sighed.

'I'm prepared to give the benefit of the doubt,' he announced abruptly. Their eyes met and something indefinable passed between them that made Kate's breathing quicken perceptibly. 'Actually, I went to school in England,' he added casually.

Kate frowned. 'Boarding school?' That suggested a privileged background, as did his autocratic manner. Had he chosen crime out of choice or had circumstances forced him down that road? It seemed a wicked shame that someone she sensed had so much potential should waste his talents.

'Do I detect a hint of disapproval?'

The edge of indulgent amusement in his voice made Kate bristle. 'Well, if I had children I wouldn't ship them away...' She encountered the interested glint in his eyes and bit her lip. Like he's *really* interested in what you'd do with your children, Kate... A sane person didn't enter into a debate on private versus state education with her abductor.

'It didn't do me any harm.'

Kate couldn't stop herself snorting derisively when he wheeled out the tired old line.

'In fact...'

'It got you where you are today—which I'd say was looking at a kidnapping charge, at the very least.'

'Does that mean if I let you go you'll run straight to the police?'

Kate's face fell as she realised her smart tongue had got her into even more trouble. 'I'm in no position to go to the police without incriminating myself.' She waited, fingers crossed, for his response.

'You being such a hardened criminal...'

Kate unable to interpret the odd inflection in his tone frowned. 'Not *hardened*, exactly... You went to school in England—does that mean you're *not* Spanish?'

'A man could be forgiven for thinking you're trying to change the subject.'

'I'm curious, that's all...'

'About my ancestry?'

'About your eyes...' She cleared her throat and blushed hotly as the dangerous glint in his eyes intensified. 'I just happened to notice they're blue,' she explained carelessly. 'It's unusual for someone with your colouring,' she added defensively.

'Yes, it is. I have a Scottish grandmother.'

'It's never too late, you know...' she heard herself blurt out suddenly.

Much to her dismay, he eased himself farther onto the bed and folded his arms comfortably across his chest. Kate had his full, undivided attention and she didn't want it!

'For what is it never too late?'

Feeling deeply embarrassed by her earnest outburst Kate rubbed her nose against the duvet and surreptitiously shuffled as far across the big bed as she could without falling off. Why can't I leave well enough alone? she wondered in exasperation. Why do I always have to try and rehabilitate hopeless cases?

'Kate's problem is she doesn't know a lost cause when she sees it,' friends had frequently observed affectionately.

'To do something else,' she muttered awkwardly. 'Something...*legal*...'

'Are you trying to reform me?' An expression of amazement, tinged by something she couldn't interpret, chased across his sternly proud face.

'It's nothing to me if you end up rotting in prison!' she countered crossly. 'Now, if you give me back my clothes, I'll just be going...'

'Just out of curiosity, what would you do if I said you couldn't go?'

Kate's expression froze. The ambivalence of her response to this taunt was deeply troubling. A person who found anything attractive or exciting about being held captive by someone like him was a candidate for the funny farm! She gulped and her throat muscles locked down tight as her eyes welded with his shimmering blue gaze. It took her a few moments before the obstruction in her throat cleared.

'If I told you, I'd lose the element of surprise.' The truth, she reasoned, could not make matters much worse at this point. 'And, from where I'm lying, that's about the only thing I have going for me,' she added with feeling.

To her amazement he threw back his dark head and laughed; it was a warm uninhibited and incredibly attractive sound.

'You have a lot more going for you than that, K. M. Anderson,' he announced caressingly.

'What's with the charm offensive?' she asked suspiciously. And if I was a weaker, more gullible girl, it might just work—because a smile like that, she reflected bitterly, ought to carry health warnings.

'Do you think all men have a hidden agenda?'

'No, just you,' she declared without thinking.

He didn't appear offended by her reply. 'I've never met a woman with your brand of candour; it is most disarming.'

He didn't look disarmed, he looked worryingly thoughtful. 'Are you going to get me my clothes?'

'If the doctor says you can get dressed, yes.'

'Doctor? What doctor...?'

On cue, there was the sound of voices just outside the bedroom door.

'This doctor.'

A man entered the room but it wasn't a doctor, it was the heavy from earlier, looking a lot less sinister—unlike his partner in crime—in proper light. He smiled at Kate and she found herself smiling back, confused by this polite, totally unthreatening individual, a million miles away from her hazy mental image of him.

She turned back to the man ensconced beside her on the bed. 'You expect me to believe you've called a doctor?' she hissed in a contemptuous undertone.

His blue eyes swept over her flushed face. 'You will naturally believe what you think,' he returned haughtily. 'However, I have arranged medical assistance.'

'I suppose a dead body would be inconvenient, even for someone like you,' she spat back.

One brow lifted at her venomous tone but didn't respond as he rose to greet his friend. It didn't occur to Javier to ask whether Serge had managed to procure the services of a doctor; Serge wasn't the sort of man who didn't complete tasks.

'That was quick, Serge.'

'I didn't need to chase up the on-call doctor. Luckily they mentioned at reception that Dr Latimer was staying overnight after a party. I woke him up.'

'He did indeed, so I hope you'll excuse my appearance.'

Kate's confusion increased as a tall, grey-haired individual panting slightly and carrying a black case followed the younger man into the room. Despite his words, he looked casually but impeccably turned out to her.

'Javier!' The older man grasped the hand extended to him, his expression warm.

'Conrad!'

Kate's initial worry that an innocent doctor had been coerced into attending under threat of violence by her unscrupulous captor was fading fast, this respectable looking individual appeared to be no stranger.

'How good to see you,' the doctor continued warmly. The subtle degree of deference in his manner added to Kate's bewilderment. 'How is your grandfather? Thinking of retiring, I hear…'

Javier just smiled noncommittally.

'Hard for a man like that to take a back seat,' the doctor observed, blind to the air of tension which Kate had immediately detected in the younger man. 'Is he doing any of the things I suggested on our last meeting?'

'You mean, has he cut back on the cigars and brandy…is he taking regular exercise and watching his diet? Did you really expect him to?'

The respected medic, who was living in semi-retirement on the island, grinned ruefully. 'My wife tells me that I'm an eternal optimist.' He caught sight of Kate, who was lying there watching the proceedings, a frown on her face as she tried to make sense of their conversation—could she have got mixed up with a member of some notorious criminal family…? And why was this Javier uncomfortable discussing his grandparent? 'Is this my patient?'

'Yes this is Miss Anderson.' Taller than the other men, his every movement lithe and co-ordinated, the dark-clad figure walked back over to the bed and touched her shoulder. Somehow his body language and tone managed an easy intimacy which she wanted immediately to deny.

'Kate took a nasty knock on the head...didn't you, sweetheart?'

If Kate blinked at this casual use of her name—she was pretty sure she hadn't revealed this detail—she almost choked over the endearment that followed.

'She lost consciousness?'

'She was out for several minutes,' he stated with the confidence of a man who didn't deal approximations. 'I don't know whether this is relevant, Conrad—' his magnificent shoulders lifted in an elegant, economic gesture—Kate, her eyes drawn against her will to the lean vital frame of the man beside her, shivered; she couldn't recall meeting anyone with such expressive body language. 'But she appears to have a temperature.'

'No, I haven't,' Kate intervened, hurriedly removing her glazed stare from the hard contours of his long, well-developed thighs. She judged it was about time she stopped lying there, meekly ogling, while they discussed her as if she wasn't there. 'And if anyone wants to know how I am, they can ask me,' she added pugnaciously.

The two men exchanged understanding glances that made Kate want to scream.

'Quite right, too,' the doctor agreed jovially, with that jarringly patronising manner his profession had perfected. He fished a pair of half-moon glasses to peer at her over from the breast pocket of his pristine shirt and she was almost amused to note that the picture of professional condescension was complete!

At least his irritating bedside manner reassured her of his authenticity; up to that point Kate had been harbouring suspicions about his identity. After all, she only had this Javier's word for it he was a doctor at all—and his word didn't inspire her trust.

'This is ludicrous. I don't need a doctor, I need—' she began, only to be smoothly interrupted.

'Don't get excited, Kate…'

Kate dragged herself higher in the bed, pinning the duvet under her chin. Under the circumstances, her restraint was nothing short of miraculous!

'You think this is excited…?' She gave a dry laugh. 'I think I've got a right to be *excited!*' she squeaked indignantly. 'And don't look at me like that,' she added shrilly.

Their eyes clashed combatively and Kate's chin went up; she considered it a matter of principle not to be the first to look away. 'I don't know what sort of women you're used to dealing with,' she began scornfully, 'but…'

The doctor cleared his throat tactfully and looked indulgently from one warring party to the other. 'Perhaps it would be better, Javier, if you left us to it?' he suggested tentatively.

The amused competitive blue eyès finally broke contact with hers.

'If you want anything, just call. We'll be…' The inclination of Javier's dark imperious head indicated the door.

Kate was suspicious of this unexpected capitulation; her frown was fielded by an improbably innocent smile.

'You must let me look at that wound on your hand afterwards, Javier. It looks as if it could do with dressing,' the doctor called after the departing men.

Kate's gaze shifted from Javier's provoking eyes to his hand at the same moment he raised it to his lips. She shifted uncomfortably and heat flooded her face as she recalled the moment she had bitten down hard. She chewed her lower lip in guilty agitation as their glances once more locked.

'I had an encounter with an angry cat,' he replied with a dismissive shrug.

'Perhaps,' Kate observed sourly, 'you provoked her…'

The doctor, oblivious to the undercurrents, commented

on the number of feral animals roaming free. 'I hope your tetanus shots are up to date, Javier,' he called as the other men began once more to withdraw.

A nod of confirmation and he was gone.

CHAPTER FOUR

THE sudden release of tension left Kate feeling limp; she couldn't believe her luck.

'Conrad Latimer,' the doctor formally introduced himself.

Kate ignored the introduction and, pushing back the duvet she swung her feet purposefully to the floor. The room began to tilt crazily. She clutched her spinning head and sprawled weakly backwards.

'I think perhaps I did that too quickly,' she murmured faintly.

'I think perhaps the fact you did it at all is the problem.'

'You don't understand I have to get out of here—*quickly!*' she fretted, frustrated that he wasn't appreciating the extreme urgency of the matter. Kate sighed. Whilst she would have preferred to appeal for help from a disinterested party, which this man obviously wasn't, she didn't have much choice. 'You're English?' she asked, in a desperate attempt to find some common ground.

'Yes. My wife and I spend most of the year in our villa on the island, since I retired; it's in a lovely spot just outside Pollensa. You must get Javier to fetch you to visit us, if he has time.'

Kate stared at him incredulously, presumably this depended on Javier having a gap in his busy schedule he could fit in this merry jaunt...somewhere between larceny and extortion, possibly? Just what sort of cosy relationship did he think she had with that wretched man? She'd never imagined herself as a gangster's moll before; it troubled her that she imagined it now.

'But enough of that, let's take a look at you.' He gently probed the tender lump on the side of her skull, Kate winced. 'I'm sorry. How did it happen?'

'Apparently I ran into a wardrobe.'

'An impetuous lady,' came the indulgent response.

'It wasn't my fault,' she began indignantly.

'No, these accidents happen—unlucky thing, certainly, but at least Javier was there—a good man in a crisis, Javier. None better...'

Kate almost choked at this unlikely description of her persecutor. 'He's very competent, certainly,' she replied grimly.

'The Monteros are all a pretty charismatic lot, but in my opinion Javier is the best of the bunch.' What bunch? Kate wanted to ask. *Javier Montero*, where had she heard that before? It definitely sounded familiar but her muzzy brain just wouldn't make the necessary connections. 'Have you known him long?' he asked, shining a penlight into her eyes.

'Not long,' she hedged. 'This might sound a bit strange, Doctor...'

'Any double vision, nausea?'

'No, but, Doctor...?'

'Yes, my dear?' He began to check her reflexes.

'Where am I?'

The doctor replaced his patella hammer in his case; he was too professional to display any overt alarm.

'Disorientation is not at all unusual after a knock like you've taken,' he soothed cautiously. 'Just what do you remember about the accident?'

'Too much,' she responded feelingly.

'And before?'

'There's nothing wrong with my memory. I just don't know where I am,' she gritted in frustration.

'You're the same place you were before the accident, I expect, my dear. The honeymoon suite at the…'

'The what?' Kate squawked, struggling upright.

'The honeymoon suite,' he repeated patiently. 'I'm sure you'll remember if you give yourself time.'

'I won't remember the honeymoon suite because I'm not staying in it. I'm not on my honeymoon… I'm in a night-mare!'

The doctor looked amused. 'Honeymoon! Well, that would make the headlines, wouldn't it?' he chuckled.

'It would…?'

Her bemused response made him laugh even more heart-ily, then abruptly the humour faded from his face. 'Don't think for a second that I'm prying. Why, I know how much Javier values his privacy, and I can see you feel the same way. Listen, your relationship with him is none of my busi-ness; you're his guest and my patient…and I can promise you that nobody will hear from me that you are staying here.'

Kate laughed at the irony of this reassurance. It was be-yond her why he felt the need to make it, but then just about everything was beyond her at that moment.

'I do not have a relationship with this Javier Montero— why, I don't even—'

'Is she in there? Katie!' The sound of a familiar lilting voice stopped Kate mid-flow.

'Mother?' she gasped incredulously. Oh, my God, that knock on the head must have been worse than I thought, she decided as she frantically tried to come up with a reason for hearing her mother's voice beside insanity.

Not too keen to reveal she was hearing things, Kate broached the subject cautiously. 'Do you hear anyone?' she asked not particularly hopefully.

Her eyes widened as the door was pushed open and the

unmistakable figure of Elizabeth Anderson rushed in—if this was an hallucination, it was a very realistic one!

'My dearest child!'

Kate, enfolded in a fragrant maternal embrace, wouldn't have dreamt of contradicting her mother, but she knew her emotional statement was not strictly accurate. Whilst Elizabeth Anderson was undoubtedly fond of both her daughters, Susie, always the more demonstrably affection-ate of the girls, was the indisputable apple of her eye.

'How did you know I was here, Mother?' she croaked bemusedly when the pressure on her ribs eased enough for her to breathe.

'Why, Javier came to get us, of course; what a lovely man he is. You naughty girl,' she remonstrated, wagging her finger with a playfulness that Kate couldn't make head nor tail of. 'Why didn't you tell us you were a...' She shot Kate a sly, knowing look from under her eyelashes that reminded Kate how similar physically Susie and their mother were. *'Friend* of Javier Montero. Why, I didn't even know you knew him!' she exclaimed with another girlish giggle that grated on Kate's frayed nerve-endings. 'I sup-pose that's why you left dinner early, to meet him...' She clicked her tongue in annoyance. 'Though why you should think all the subterfuge was necessary is beyond me... It's not as if we'd object, is it?' She laughed heartily at the notion. 'Not that you've ever worried about my feelings before.' A note of misuse entered in her voice.

'You're *pleased* I know him?' Kate echoed in a strangled voice.

'Katherine Mary Anderson, I wonder about you some-times, child. The Monteros must be one of the wealthiest families in Europe!' she exclaimed in a scandalised tone.

'Oh, my God!' Kate breathed faintly as enlightenment dawned in blinding splendour. The mental leap required to transfer Javier from her mental file marked 'member of the shady underworld' to one marked 'member of a rich and powerful dynasty that could trace its origins back centuries' left her reeling.

'You always were a sly, secretive child.' She heard Elizabeth reflect in a long-suffering manner. 'You and your father, always so serious about something or other, but he swears he didn't know either… Is it true? Haven't you told him?'

'Told him what?'

Ignoring her daughter's shaky query, Elizabeth looked admiringly around the room. 'The *honeymoon suite*,' her mother exclaimed, in a voice loaded with significance.

Honeymoon suite—oh, God! Being familiar with the way her mother's mind worked, Kate could see where she was going. Marriage was the only career any woman needed, in her mother's eyes, and a woman who hadn't snagged her man by thirty was a failure. Much to Kate's relief, her frustrated parent had written her off before she'd reached that milestone and concentrated her efforts instead on her more malleable sibling.

'Mum, please don't read anything into that!' Kate pleaded. 'I had an accident; this was the most convenient place…'

With a display of selective deafness that was her forte, Elizabeth continued to examine the décor. 'Very impressive and extremely tasteful,' came her final verdict. 'And that Jacuzzi in the deck overlooking the sea, it's just like the one your father and I had when we were in Jamaica last year. Isn't it marvellous to lie there and listen to the waves?'

At that moment Kate could think of worse things than her hot, sticky body being immersed in cool water. She dwelt dreamily for a moment on an image of her naked body being caressed by the soft water, no sounds—especially not her mother's voice—but that of the sea. It was very soothing, until her fertile and wayward imagination added a disruptive element to the picture in the shape of… Perhaps it wasn't such a good idea to think about shapes, she decided, as images of long, glistening, lean limbs and taut masculine muscles floated around suggestively in her head. Suffice it to say, she wasn't alone in the tub! Her heart began to thud frantically against her ribcage as she shook her head to blank out the depraved activities her illusionary couple were indulging in.

Elizabeth turned, with a charming smile that could still dazzle, to the doctor. 'How is she, doctor?' she asked casting a critical eye over her glassy-eyed eldest born. 'She looks a bit strange to me…'

Strange! If this indeed wasn't some strange and bizarre nightmare from which she would awaken any moment, then the man she'd taken for a sinister crime lord was actually a prominent member of the legendary family whose business interests spanned the globe! A family whose marriages to equally newsworthy individuals made front page in newspapers from New York to Istanbul.

Naturally this put his presence in the blackmailer's room in an entirely different light; unlike her, he'd obviously been there legitimately. On top of all that, her mind was filled with steamy images of herself doing things she'd never even imagined before, and despite the suffocating heat her burning nipples were brazenly protruding through the flimsy fabric of her bra!

'It's awfully warm in here…' If she had ever felt this mortified or confused in her life before, Kate was pretty sure she'd have remembered!

'Actually, I was just wondering why the air conditioning is working full blast in here?'

Kate cast a startled look in the doctor's direction and was worried when his nod confirmed her mother's assessment.

'Miss Anderson has taken a nasty knock on the head,' he began to explain. 'I think peace, quiet and rest are the best things I can prescribe for that…'

Wearily, Kate shot him a pathetically grateful look; as much as she loved her mother, even at the best of times a conversation with her could be an exhausting experience…and her head did ache so…

'I'd like her to have an X-ray, just to be on the safe side. Javier will arrange that, no doubt. My main concern is the fever she's running…'

'I have a fever!' Kate exclaimed.

'You do indeed. Your throat is red and inflamed and your lymph nodes are enlarged, which is a sure sign of infection.'

Kate, who had been too occupied by foiling blackmailers and evading kidnappers to wonder about something as mundane as the feelings of general malaise afflicting her, felt beneath her jaw and encountered the tender area he was speaking of.

'It's probably a virus,' he continued. 'Maybe just the twenty-four hour variety…?'

Kate smiled back at him, approving his optimistic attitude.

'Have you been in contact with anyone with flu or anything of that nature?'

Elizabeth Anderson got up hurriedly from the bedside, regarding her daughter with reproachful horror.

'No, I don't think so…' Kate began; then she recalled the baby on the flight. 'There was this child on the flight over, I had him on my knee and he was a bit grizzly…you know, hot and snuffly.'

The doctor nodded. 'That could well be the explanation. The cramped conditions on planes make it a fertile breeding ground for bugs. On the other hand, it might be quite unrelated.'

'Really, Kate, that's so like you,' her mother complained, delicately examining her own neck. 'You never stop to think about how your actions affect others. This is your father's first break for months; how are you going to feel if he becomes ill because of your thoughtlessness?'

Kate accepted the strictures meekly. 'Sorry...'

'And I shall complain to the airline. You pay for a first class ticket—'

'Well, actually,' Kate admitted guiltily, 'I was travelling economy.'

Kate wasn't surprised when her mother looked appalled. Elizabeth was a terrible snob who went to great pains to disguise her own working-class roots. *'Economy!'*

'I didn't think Dad would mind if I traded in my ticket and put the money towards the deposit for my new flat,' she added defensively.

Kate, tired of flat-sharing and determined to enter the property market, had been economising wherever possible during the last year. She didn't know how people in less well-paid jobs than herself managed in the scarily pricey London property market.

'Are you decent? Can I come in?'

Kate welcomed the interruption as her father's round, cheery face peered cautiously around the door—Charles Anderson, with his cherubic countenance, did not look like most people's image of a sober judge. *'Dad!* Come in...*please!'* she added, with a harassed glance in her mother's direction.

After first assuring himself his daughter didn't look near death's door, Charles Anderson smiled. 'Well, what have you been up to, pumpkin?' he began heartily as he approached Kate's bedside, his arms extended.

Kate blinked, embarrassed by the way her eyes filled weakly with tears at the casual endearment; Dad hadn't called her that for years.

'Charles, don't go near her, she's infectious!' his wife shrieked in alarm.

'Nonsense, Lizzie, since when was a knock on the head infectious?' Charles Anderson returned, dismissing his wife's appeal.

Kate on the other hand, saw the good sense in what her mother was saying; she certainly had no desire to ruin everyone else's holiday.

'Actually, Dad...' she stopped, losing track of her train of thought as her attention was fatally distracted by the figure silently entering the room behind her father.

The younger man had to be at least six four or five to be able to dwarf Charles Anderson's burly figure. His autocratic air might make sense now but it didn't make it any less obnoxious to Kate.

As a man born to wield power, Javier Montero certainly fulfilled all the criteria. He was arrogant, overbearing and insufferably rude. An unashamed aristocrat, who smugly imagined an accident of birth gave him special rights and privileges, decided the woman who made a point of never judging people on appearances!

Mentally pulling his character to shreds gave her a temporary respite from examining in any depth the worrying fact she found his presence electrifying.

Kate wasn't the sort of person who normally had a problem laughing at herself or her mistakes when the circumstances warranted it, but there were limits! When she thought about how terrified she'd been, her blood boiled. No doubt he'd been having a laugh at her expense all night.

Amongst the things she'd said that made her squirm now, the recollection of the earnest advice she'd given him on reforming his criminal life stood out as particularly cringeworthy!

Kate constructively converted her embarrassment to anger as she glared with distrust and dislike at Javier's distinguished profile. Why the hell hadn't he just come out and explained who he was, like any normal person, instead of letting her blather on and on?

Javier wasn't surprised by the to-hell-with-you look in those velvety exotically slanted eyes as they met his—head on, of course. He'd already worked out that K. M. Anderson was an impetuous, head-on sort of female. This characteristic made her very different from most of the women he knew, women who often said what they imagined he wanted to hear. Though there was nothing remotely predatory about this Kate—in fact, if anything, she gave the impression of being unaware of her own attractiveness—she was undoubtedly intelligent and strong-willed.

As much as he admired these traits, Javier wasn't normally sexually attracted to women who possessed them. Perhaps the allure in this case had something to do with the fact these characteristics came wrapped in the sort of body he'd always admired—athletic without being muscular, curvaceous without being lush, he decided appreciatively as his eyes skimmed her recumbent form.

He acknowledged her antagonism with the very faintest of wry smiles that suggested to the seething Kate he was enjoying every second of her discomfort.

Childishly determined not to be the first to look away, she didn't know how long the silent eye-to-eye combat continued, but she was relieved and immensely grateful when Conrad Latimer's timely intervention gave her a legitimate excuse to look away.

'It seems likely that your daughter, Mr Anderson, has a viral infection of some sort to go with a mild concussion.'

'Caught no doubt from the horrid child she nursed all the way over in the plane,' Elizabeth clarified with a disapproving sniff.

'Always the soft touch, hey, Katie,' her father remarked fondly as, ignoring his wife's remonstrations, he hugged his daughter. 'Feeling pretty rotten…?' He straightened up and tugged one limp strand of blonde hair as he keenly surveyed his eldest daughter's pale face.

Now she wasn't looking at the elegant, tall figure oozing more vitality than seemed decent for one individual, Kate's breathing had almost settled to a normal rhythm.

'Not too bad, Dad.'

Javier, who had been conversing with the doctor in a soft undertone, stepped quietly forwards. It required no dramatic gestures to make his lean, dynamic figure the focus of attention; Kate found herself admiring his sheer presence even as she resented it.

She watched as he inclined his head courteously towards her mother, who looked bowled over by this old-fashioned display—though Kate suspected that her mother was so disgustingly impressed by his financial and social position it would take a lot to make her look upon him with anything but fawning approval! She watched his display with a cynical smile. Oh, no doubt about it, his company manners were second to none, she brooded, but having been on the receiving end of his anger she could have told them about another less pleasant side to his nature… Big bully!

'You'll wish to stay with your daughter no doubt, Mrs Anderson. I'm afraid for obvious reasons there is no second bedroom in this suite.' This comment elicited a flurry of smiles. 'But I'll arrange for a bed to be brought in here…or would you prefer it in the sitting room…?'

'Oh! Oh no, we couldn't possibly put you to so much trouble…'

Kate saw her mother's dilemma straight off; she also saw the cynical twist of Javier's lips as he listened politely to the older woman bluster.

If Elizabeth hadn't been so loath to appear anything but the caring mother in this man's eyes, she'd have recoiled in horror at the idea of playing nurse. Kate knew that anything to do with illness spooked her mother—especially the possibility she might become ill herself! Fortunately, other than her scald, both she and Susie had been extremely healthy children. But her burns had been bad and had left a lasting impact on Kate—and a dislike of hospitals.

'I'd much prefer to go back to my own room,' she put in hurriedly. 'I'm feeling much better.'

'Kate doesn't like to be fussed when she's ill,' her father explained to Javier. 'But do you think it's such a good idea going back to your own room, Kate? If Susie catches something, we'll all be...!' His bushy brows which met over the bridge of his nose arched expressively.

'*God, no!*' Kate exclaimed immediately. 'I can't do that.' Susie, like their mother, was not the most stoic of patients; she never suffered alone! 'And I don't want to pass this bug on to the other guests.'

'You will naturally stay here as long as necessary, Kate.'

The way he said her name made Kate's skin prickle—not a good sign. She just hoped it was antipathy and nothing more sinister that was responsible for this sensation! She longed to refuse the offer on more than one count—firstly all her instincts told her to disagree in principle with anything this wretched man said, secondly she desperately didn't want to be beholden with him, and last, but not least, she could sense her mother putting two and two together and coming up with an unhealthy five!

Kate tensed. If Mum starts dropping heavy hints of a matrimonial nature, I'll kill her, she vowed. Better that, though, she reflected worriedly, than seeing her blatant matchmaking mother annihilated by one of the cutting barbs she was sure Javier was more than capable of delivering!

'Now that's what I call a generous offer,' Charles Anderson said, looking mightily relieved. 'Isn't it, Kate?'

Kate smiled in a sickly way back at him and tried unsuccessfully to resist the mesmeric pull of mocking blue eyes—she failed miserably. Chin up, she glared, ignoring that sinking sensation low in her belly; whilst she was in no position to throw his offer back in his face, she could at least make sure he knew that's what she'd like to do!

'It's the least I can do, under the circumstances,' he responded smoothly.

'You bet it is!' Aware of the stares that her spiky retort had caused, Kate forced herself to smile. She gritted her teeth through the horridly bright grimace and fantasised about puncturing his ego—it was a healthier fantasy than others she'd indulged in recently.

'Yes, very kind,' she responded stiffly.

CHAPTER FIVE

IT SEEMED like hours to Kate before the room finally emptied and she was left alone. She waited until she heard the door click closed with a sound of promising finality before leaving her bed to search for the bathroom. Her need was fairly urgent and the search proved to be frustratingly slow.

'Never a loo when you need one,' she grumbled softly to herself as the first two doors she opened turned out to be walk-in wardrobes. She was about to try out the third when a voice at her shoulder almost made her leap out of her skin.

'You should not be out of bed.'

Hand pressed to her thundering heart, she spun around, an action which made her head spin as she tilted it back to look up at the tall man towering over her.

'You're gone…!'

Even before one dark brow rose, Kate was wincing at the inanity of this patently false observation, because he definitely was very much there!

Every lean, muscle-packed inch of Javier Montero was standing so close that, had she chosen to reach out, she could have touched him—touched his broad chest, his lean flat belly. In fact, had she wanted to touch him, like a child in a sweet shop she'd have been spoilt for choice!

Kate swallowed hard and averted her eyes before she was totally submerged by the wave of sensual inertia that washed over her. She might no longer fear for her life in his presence but she wasn't so sure about her sanity. This man's raw masculinity had roughly the same effect as a thousand volts of unearthed electricity on her nerves.

'I thought you were asleep.'

What would it be like, she found herself speculating, to wake up and find that face on the pillow beside you when you woke up? She swallowed convulsively, further unsettled by the alarming direction of her maverick thoughts. Aware that his heavy-lidded eyes were sliding thoughtfully over the length of her body, she folded her arms defensively over her chest and felt extremely glad she'd taken the time to exchange the slinky black undies for the pretty nightdress which was beautifully cool on her overheated body and, more importantly, given her present situation, covered her from neck to ankle.

It was doubtful she would have considered this a fortuitous exchange had she realised that, despite the demure design and sweet embroidered flowers around the scooped neckline, the borrowed nightdress was totally transparent beneath the electric light!

'So you just thought you'd, what...? Come and watch me?' Now there was a *very* unsettling thought. 'Have you been demoted to nursemaid, or has making money got boring?'

'If you'd agreed to be transferred to the clinic overnight, as the doctor suggested, I wouldn't need to...'

She may not have been in a position to explain to her parents and the doctor why Javier's hospitality was neither kind nor acceptable, but she was not willingly going to actively participate in the debate over her healthcare options. Once, however, she had realised that the possibility of her being transferred to some posh clinic or other—in her eyes, a hospital was a hospital!—was being mooted, Kate become animated for as long as it took her to make it abundantly clear to everyone that, short of hog-tying or sectioning her under the Majorcan equivalent of the Mental Health Act, there was no way she was going to any plush private clinic!

'And as for CT scans and skull X-rays, I won't have one!' she had explained firmly.

When she'd heard her father begin to apologetically explain away her unreasonable behaviour with a discreet reference to the numerous operations and skin grafts she'd bravely endured as a child, Kate had cut him short with a glare so ferocious he'd not attempted to continue. Her hospital phobia, well-known to those who knew her best, was not something she wanted revealing to a man like Javier Montero.

'Spend a night in hospital for a bump on the head...? *Nonsense!*' she contended stubbornly.

'*Bumps* on the head have been known to have serious consequences...and I do feel indirectly responsible for your injury...'

'With damn good reason—you are responsible!'

'The doctor told me to watch out for irrational behaviour. Help me out here... Is this the norm for you, or should I start worrying?'

'Very funny! You're a laugh a minute, not to mention a regular ray of sunshine!' she snorted. 'I suppose you're just hanging around in the hope I'll take a turn for the worse? Well, sorry to disappoint you; I'm feeling fine,' she lied.

Though he didn't respond as such to her childish retort, he still managed with just a look to make her feel petty and churlish. 'No, you're not. As I've already told you, I feel partially responsible for your injuries and, besides, who else was there? Your mother?'

'Leave my mother out of this... Not everyone makes a good nurse,' Kate defended hotly. 'And even if I needed one, which I don't, you wouldn't be it!'

'Possibly not, but as it happens I'm all you have, and fortunately I have an extremely robust immune system; I don't get ill...'

Listening to this complacent pronouncement, Kate

couldn't help but uncharitably wish he'd contract something nasty, not dangerously so—she wasn't a malicious girl—but bad enough to turn that aristocratic nose red and make those glorious electric-blue eyes watery and red-rimmed.

'Pity!' It was deeply frustrating to discover her vicious comment merely seemed to amuse him. Beyond amusement there was a flicker of something else—something she couldn't quite identify, that moved behind his eyes and made her vaguely uneasy. 'I thought people like you clicked your fingers and minions came to do your bidding.'

One dark brow arched. 'People like me?'

'The disgustingly rich and idle.'

'Wealth is relative. Many would not think your upbringing impoverished; many more might even infer you would not have achieved the success you have if you hadn't had the—'

'What do you know about my achievements?' she flared angrily.

'Your parents are extremely proud of you...'

Kate's eyes widened with almost comic dismay. She could see it all, Dad rabbiting on in a besotted way about his clever daughter. God, how embarrassing...!

'My father is, you mean.' Kate instantly regretted she'd allowed him to goad her in to making this revealing observation.

'No, your mother would prefer you to marry well, I think.'

Someone like you, she almost flung, before caution intervened. 'And I suppose *well,* to you, means someone with loads of money...'

'No I think that's what it means to your mother,' he returned, a shade of impatience entering his voice. 'It offends you to be judged on anything other than merit, doesn't it?'

Kate nodded. 'Of course it does!' She knew she'd had more advantages than many people, but she'd worked damned hard to get where she was and had never traded on her father's reputation, despite the fact it could have opened many doors for her.

'Yet you do not hesitate to judge me? You have a fine legal mind; do you not detect a certain inconsistency in your attitude…?'

Kate would have walked on hot coals before she'd have acknowledged the compelling justice of this stinging rebuke; she felt herself colour under his ironic gaze.

'Incidentally,' he drawled, 'I dislike inactivity; it bores me…'

Despite his languid tone, Kate could readily believe that; the man before her was not a relaxing person. It was impossible to imagine spending an evening curled up contentedly on a sofa beside him, watching an old film on telly, and not just because it was highly unlikely he'd ask someone like her; he exuded a restless vitality the like of which she'd never encountered before.

'I do beg your pardon,' she drawled crankily. 'Rich and active.'

'Aren't we rather losing track of the point here? Leaving my bank balance aside for one moment, the doctor did specifically say that you should stay in bed until the morning.'

'Slight problem there—I need the bathroom—*now!*' she revealed with malicious relish—such a statement was sure to dismay this fastidious individual. She was disappointed.

Head tilted slightly to one side, in a gesture she was starting to recognised as characteristic of him, Javier appeared to consider this blunt announcement calmly for a moment before he nodded his head in a manner Kate supposed was the equivalent hereabouts of gracious Royal approval.

'You might own the place,' she grouched, 'but I think

you'll find yourself on shaky legal ground when it comes to wandering uninvited into guests' bedrooms.' Perhaps this wasn't the most gracious response from someone who was occupying a swish suite, courtesy of the management, but Kate was too rattled by his presence to be polite about the intrusion.

'Perhaps we should discuss the legal definition of trespass after you have…erm…availed yourself of the facilities?' he suggested smoothly. 'Next door down,' he added, a sharp tilt of his head indicating the direction she needed to take.

Kate sniffed her disgruntled agreement. 'Everywhere I go he's there!' she grumbled darkly to herself in a voice just about loud enough for him to hear. 'Anyone would think you liked me…' *You wish…!*

His blue eyes dropped to the lush outline of her parted lips. 'Would that be so extraordinary?'

The husky rasp in his voice, combined with the scorching regard, had Kate diving through the door. She heard the sound of his husky amused laugh and her chin went up. Eyes narrowed, she poked her head out from behind the door.

'Yes!' she yelled succinctly before ducking back inside and slamming the door behind her.

Leaning heavily against the wall, waiting for her breathing to slow, she was alarmed to discover a silly grin on her face—anyone would think she enjoyed exchanging insults with the awful man.

A few minutes later, when she emerged from the bathroom, she discovered him lounging indolently in a leather easy chair he'd pulled up to the bedside. He got to his feet as she approached and poured a glass of iced water from the full jug that had appeared magically on her bedside table.

'Plenty of fluids, I believe the doctor said, and maybe

the robe is not such a good idea,' he murmured as she climbed back into bed, still muffled in the thick ankle-length robe she'd pulled on when she'd seen her reflection in the mirrored bathroom wall.

'You might have told me...' she hissed indignantly.

'Told you what?' he asked guilelessly.

As if he didn't know. 'That the damned thing was transparent!' she choked. Not coy about her body, it wasn't the fact that someone had accidentally got an eyeful...it was *who* had received it that had made her duck her head under the cold water tap until she could hold her breath no longer.

'I didn't look.'

The virtuous announcement wrenched a laugh from Kate's throat—so the man had a sense of humour after all. 'This is no laughing matter,' she retorted sternly.

'I wasn't laughing,' he reminded her gently.

Kate decided to anticipate his next inevitable observation. 'But I expect you saw enough to know it isn't me in the photos.' There was no way her trim but unremarkable figure could be mistaken for the celestial vision revealed in the grainy photos.

'Ah, the photographs.' He shrugged. 'The unusual hair colouring did mislead me initially.' His glance lingered on the freshly dampened strands that clung to her face and dripped wetly down her neck. 'But I had already come to the conclusion you were not the model.'

Of course, the figure in the photos didn't have any scars—how slow am I...? 'Pity you didn't catch on *before* you treated me like some sort of cheap tart!' The memory of his stinging contempt still rankled.

'I wasn't the only one guilty of jumping to the wrong conclusions,' he reminded her drily.

As if I could forget Kate thought, shifting uncomfortably as she reviewed with a mental shudder the whole humiliating incident.

'I only thought what you wanted me to?' she countered belligerently. 'It suited your purposes very well to have me scared stiff of you, didn't it?' she accused astutely.

'On occasion, a little bit of fear can expedite matters,' he agreed.

Kate wasn't surprised to see a total lack of remorse in his manner—the man was clearly without principles!

'However,' he continued seamlessly, 'it was obvious from the outset that you are a difficult person to intimidate...'

'An expert on intimidation, are you?'

Far from insulting him, her acid retort only made him look modestly smug. Kate gritted her teeth in frustration; if she hadn't experienced the frightening impact of his raw anger first-hand she wouldn't have believed it was possible to break through that urbane mask. Put him in the witness stand, she brooded darkly, and he'd be every lawyer's nightmare!

'It didn't take an expert at anything to figure out that you are not the sort of woman who would allow herself to be compromised in that way.'

Was that a backhanded compliment or an insult too subtle for her to figure out? Kate puzzled suspiciously. Her candid gaze, which had frequently in the past unnerved the boldest of adversaries, faltered; only by gathering all her mental resources did she maintain eye contact.

'I take it,' she replied finally, 'you still have them—the photos.'

'They are safe,' he confirmed with infuriating caution.

A frown marred the smooth sweep of her forehead as she fought to retain her shaky composure. 'They're mine.' She was unable to prevent the edge of desperation creeping into her belligerent claim.

His keen eyes scanned her tense, strained features. 'We'll discuss this in the morning when you are rested and hopefully feeling less feverish,' he announced, in the manner of someone who was accustomed to having his every suggestion treated as if it was inscribed in stone. 'I'll be in the sitting room, should you require anything; I have some paperwork to attend to. Do not hesitate—'

'We'll discuss it now!' Kate cut shrilly into his formal declaration; if she fell for this phoney concerned line she'd start forgetting who the enemy was.

Javier scanned her flushed agitated face thoughtfully. 'That is probably not a good idea.'

'As it happens, I don't give a damn what you consider a good idea,' she revealed. The biting scorn of her delivery was spoiled by the weak little wobble in her voice.

'As you wish,' he replied, resuming his seat beside the bed. 'I'm assuming you were acting as an agent for…whom exactly…when you broke into that room? The person in the photos? Your sister?'

Kate's tone became increasingly desperate as she sensed herself being pushed into a corner. 'I didn't break in; the door was open…' She might as well have saved her breath; brushed aside her feeble protest with a lofty gesture.

Javier took her lack of denial concerning the identity as confirmation of his suspicions. 'And she was being blackmailed by Gonzalez? He was her lover?'

Kate released a fractured gasp. 'He's not her lover,' she denied. 'He tricked her…maybe even—' She stopped, dismay washing over her as she realised her response had only confirmed Susie's identity. 'How did you…?' she began.

'It hardly required a giant leap to reach these conclusions. Listening to your parents' conversation, it was clear that your sister is somewhat indulged… The sort of person who would send someone else to do her dirty work.'

Kate would have given a lot to have denied this scarily accurate assessment.

'You know nothing about our family situation,' she protested gruffly.

'True,' he conceded, his eyes fixed on his own long interlaced fingers not her face. 'But sometimes families are not so very different.' The curtain of long dark lashes lifted and Kate briefly saw the shadow of something that looked like deep sorrow; it was there so briefly she couldn't decide if she had imagined it or not.

'Take the robe off,' he urged, revealing an unexpected smile of extraordinary charm which lightened his sombre, clean-cut features dramatically and left Kate's lungs fighting to replace the air she had expelled in one startled gasp. When he chose to display it, he had charisma that was off the scale. 'Before you spike a fever once more, for which I will no doubt be blamed.'

'I am a little tired,' she conceded reluctantly.

'Bruised, battered and bone-weary would be nearer the mark, I suspect.'

She should have found this concern coming from the very person she held accountable for her plight a theme for her scorn, but bizarrely she found his consideration and his accented deep tone oddly soothing. Frowning, Kate puzzled over her bizarre response as she slid her arms out of the robe beneath a modestly adjusted duvet.

Her own actions paled into insignificance beside the truly bizarre thing her suspicious sideways stare then revealed. The amazing sight of Javier Montero rearranging her pillows could safely be positioned in the extreme end of bizarre—just about where it started nudging surreal!

He seemed to perform the task most proficiently for a rich playboy.

'Comfortable?' he asked as she collapsed weakly back against them.

Kate nodded, her eyelids felt heavy and it was hard to focus on his dark face. 'If I told anyone you just did that they'd never believe me...' she observed, unable to stifle a jaw-cracking yawn. 'Don't worry, I'm not likely to do so...tell anyone, that is,' she added swiftly, in case he thought him shaking her pillows was something she might want to boast about in future.

His compelling gaze swept her face—Kate could only imagine what she looked like after the trauma of the evening.

'I'm not worried,' he revealed enigmatically before leaving.

A sleepily disarmed and confused Kate was just drifting off to sleep in the quiet of the bedroom when she realised that she still hadn't regained possession of the photographs for Susie.

'In the morning,' she promised herself out loud.

CHAPTER SIX

WHEN Kate awoke, the strands of golden light filtering through the wooden shutters had cast a dappled pattern over the wall beside the bed. For a while she lay there, watching the shifting pattern.

Arm curved above her head, her fingertips brushed across the carved headboard as she stretched languidly; the vast carved bed and fine linen were deliciously decadent. The enervating languor lasted approximately twenty seconds, right up to the point where her memories of the previous night came flooding back.

Why did it have to happen to me...?

Not a person inclined to wallow, she only indulged her self-pitying reflections for a few moments. By the time she turned her head towards the tantalising, nose-twitching smell and had discovered an attractively presented tray set beside the big bed, Kate was in a more pragmatic and positive frame of mind.

She was going to get Susie's photos back and then get on with the rest of her much-needed holiday, her encounter with Javier Montero completely forgotten. An image of his dark, devastatingly attractive features flashed through her head—well, perhaps not *completely*, but he would soon be a nasty memory.

To her surprise Kate discovered she was hungry—very hungry. This had to be a good sign, didn't it?

A few cautious stretches confirmed that most of the aches and pains from the previous night had gone, and when she rotated her head it thankfully no longer felt as though a miniature percussionist was pounding away inside her skull. Whatever bug had made her feel so awful seemed to have succumbed to her own immune system.

There was plenty to appease her healthy hunger and on reflection there didn't seem any danger of placing herself any deeper in Javier's debt by accepting this hospitality. As she surveyed the food she tried with only partial success not to wonder about who might have placed her breakfast there while she lay sleeping. Had Javier kept vigil the entire night or had he delegated the task? The latter seemed much more likely.

Trying to dispel the persistent image in her head of him watching her as she slept, Kate picked up a roll from the selection of breads; it was warm and just asking to be covered with lashings of the golden butter and honey that lay beside it. Her dry mouth watered at the sight of the pot of coffee set beside the comprehensive assortment of fresh fruit. Lifting the cover from the plate, she discovered a plate of fluffy scrambled eggs; with a fork she speared a sliver of smoked salmon from the mound and found it delicious.

Kate had showered, but was still dressing in the clothes she'd been amazed to discover folded neatly over the back of a chair in the bathroom, when she heard sounds coming from the adjoining room. The clothes fitted very well, but then they would; Kate had only purchased the pale green wrap around skirt and halter neck top the previous week.

She was sliding her feet into the soft leather open-toed mules—also new—when there was an extra loud rattle. Either someone was very noisy or they were tactfully letting her know she wasn't alone... She decided this ruled out Javier, who hadn't so far shown any sign of possessing either tact or delicacy!

Despite her conviction that it wasn't him, Kate couldn't help but wish, as she surveyed her pale face in the mirror, that her small make-up bag had been included with her other cosmetics. Not that, having been blessed with a creamy, flawless complexion and naturally dark lashes, she wore anything in the summer but a natural-looking lip-gloss and the occasional dusting of eyeshadow.

Kate would have strongly rebuffed any suggestion that this desire to don face-paint had anything to do with any underlying motive on her part to impress anyone—especially if the *anyone* in question was Javier Montero. This was about feeling confident and, call her shallow, but like most women a coat of lippy could make her feel more assured, and when dealing with an unknown quantity like Javier Montero she needed all the help she could get!

She caught sight of her femininely curved behind in the mirror and the defiant set of her shoulders relaxed as a rueful smile spread across her mobile features. Who am I kidding? Of course I'd like to knock him dead; who wouldn't?

It wasn't going to happen outside her dreams though because, truth told, unlike Susie and similarly blessed females, she simply wasn't endowed with the equipment to impress that way.

'I hope you didn't lock the bathroom door.'

Javier must have very acute hearing, she thought, because he had his back turned to her so couldn't have seen her cautiously entering the bedroom.

He sounded irritated. Not the most auspicious of beginnings, she thought in dismay. Still, if he was as fed up with her as his broad back suggested—what an extraordinarily expressive anatomy he had, she marvelled, momentarily diverted by the shape of his broad, splendidly muscled shoulders and strong straight spine.

Though this started off as an innocently innocuous line of thought, somewhere between his trim waist and snaky hips it took a sharp detour into a lot less virtuous territory, anatomically speaking!

Wrenching free from this downward mental spiral, Kate took a deep breath and began again—distracting anatomical observations strictly banned this time around!

He must be fed up with her; she'd been nothing but a nuisance to him. It stood to reason that he might feel inclined to hand over the photos without any fuss just to get shot of her.

The harsh scowl revealed on his lean, saturnine features as he turned around confirmed her assumption he was not in the best of moods. Standing there, gazing at her critically over long, steepled fingers, she discovered that the man looked much more remote than her overnight mental image of him, and, in a different way, even more threatening than the criminal she had once taken him for.

Whatever else he was, this man was spectacular, she conceded as her heart began to race so frantically it felt as if it might explode from her tight chest any moment. He also had more moods and faces than anyone she'd ever met!

Kate felt no desire to delve beneath the surface of this obviously complex man; superficial details were causing her enough problems, she decided, averting her gaze from the faint shadow of dark body hair she could see through the classic white shirt tucked into a pair of tailored pale linen trousers he wore this morning. Nothing about his vital, arresting figure suggested he hadn't had an uneventful eight hours sleep.

No doubt he was one of those tiresome types who could survive indefinitely on cat naps and coffee, whereas she needed her full eight hours to function at all.

His steely, sweeping scrutiny left her with the vague impression that he found her appearance in some way lacking.

A burst of antagonism made her skin prickle. *So what? Since when did it matter to me,* she challenged herself, *that some man didn't like my outfit?* It was plain daft to feel aggrieved; he was entitled to his opinion, just like she was entitled not to give a damn!

My appearance is probably a bit of a shock, she reflected contemptuously. He probably doesn't appreciate that it takes the glamorous types he wakes up next to ninety per cent of their time to look that way. These women dedicated to looking beautiful had almost certainly spoilt him for ordinary women like herself.

Fortunately she had never been attracted to the smouldering Southern Mediterranean type.

He could exploit his sexual magnetism for all it was worth; she wasn't going to be distracted. She had to stay focused! Think more about Susie and less about his stern, sensual mouth.

Her chin tilted to an aggressive angle that reflected her militant frame of mind she sauntered across the room.

'If you think this is bad, you should have seen me before the shower!' she snapped with a toss of her head.

Javier had.

He over the years had a number of lovers, but he was not in the habit of spending the entire night with them; perhaps that was why her face in repose had fascinated him so much. He judged it possibly wasn't a good idea, considering her overt hostility, to share these details with her.

'Have I done something to offend you?'

Other than look so damned superior? 'I didn't care for your tone.' Kate didn't care for the gleam of amusement in his eyes as he watched her progression across the room, either.

'You have something against Spanish accents?'

'No, just bossy men of any nationality.' She had no intention of revealing that she found his accent extremely attractive; the velvet rasp of his slightly foreign syllables sent forbidden little shivers down her spine.

'I didn't lock the door...'

She bent her head forwards and shook out her damp hair, teasing the knots in the silken threads with her fingers and showering his immaculate person with wet droplets. Throwing her head back she intercepted an expression in his eyes that almost made her lose her composure—imagined or real, the sensual heat of that fleeting look made her stomach collapse inwards.

'But if I'd known you were in here I definitely would have!' she boasted huskily.

One ebony brow arched expressively. He didn't appear impressed by this slightly desperate display of how unintimidated she was by him—but then it was hard to establish indifference when your voice quivered and shook.

'And if you'd collapsed?'

Well aware she didn't have a leg to stand on, she responded to this common-sense observation with a disdainful toss of her head.

'As you can see.' She held her arms wide and performed a graceful twirl for his benefit. 'I'm fit and well,' she finished triumphantly as her billowing skirts settled back around the long line of her thighs. 'Not a wobble in sight,' she lied cheerfully.

She'd have felt a lot more like smiling if the fact her head was spinning crazily had something to do with the manoeuvre or her weakened condition, but it didn't; it was breathing the same air as this wretched man that turned her into some sort of hormonal junkie!

'No headache, no ache and pains. In fact I'm absolutely fine.'

He picked up a peach from her breakfast tray and bit into the soft flesh.

A sigh snagged in Kate's throat; the fruit had left a faint film of moisture on the sensual outline of his lips, and her stomach muscles spasmed viciously.

'Before you cartwheel around the room...' Javier dwelt

indulgently for a split second on the image of her cart-wheeling around the room in that skirt, so demure, but in-clined, even when cartwheels were not involved, to expose intriguing glimpses of creamy thigh.

Kate intercepting the direction of his fixed stare glanced down, wondering if she had a blob of toothpaste or some-thing on her skirt that had offended his fastidious senses. She smoothed the fabric with her hand but couldn't see anything amiss. When she looked back up his gaze was now fixed on her face, his expression impassive, though there was a curious dark line of colour along the crests of his sharp sculpted cheekbones.

'...Or do fifty push-ups, possibly? I feel I should point out I am quite prepared to accept the fact you were suffer-ing from a twenty-four hour bug and concussion. Your mother—' he shook his dark head slowly from side to side. 'Now that might be a different story. I suspect she won't be satisfied by anything less than a medical certificate and a week's quarantine...and your sister, I got the impression earlier that she was quite happy to have you stay here.'

Kate's face fell as she was struck by the accuracy of his observation. Her mother was not the sort of person to ex-pose herself to the risk of infection, no matter how minus-cule that risk might be.

'You saw Susie?'

Javier had seen many *Susies* and this one had made as little lasting impression as the others. For his money, this sister was much more memorable. The sort of woman his grandfather would consider had fire; he was pleased to see that, true to her word, she didn't try and hide those insig-nificant scars, which to his mind only emphasised the creamy perfection of the rest of her smooth skin.

At a moment when Kate had rarely felt less composed, she would have been astonished to learn that he was ad-miring her confidence.

He inclined his head. 'A temperature of one hundred and two didn't keep you in bed, so I doubted if doctor's orders or myself would have better luck today. I thought you might like to wear your own things this morning. I must say, you look quite charming...'

Kate was dismayed to find herself shifting awkwardly from foot to foot and colouring up hotly like a schoolgirl at the unexpected but slick compliment.

'If it wasn't for the bruise...'

Kate forced herself not to retreat as he moved unexpectedly forwards and, lifting up her fringe, ran a fingertip gently over the discolorated area on her temple.

'You wouldn't know anything had happened. Sorry,' he apologised as she caught her breath sharply.

Kate nodded her head and smoothed her hair back down as his hand fell away. She wasn't about to reveal, not even if her life depended on it, that pain had had nothing to do with her response. The stab of sharp sexual awareness that had jolted through her body at his touch made further self-deception on her part futile.

She ran the tip of her tongue over her dry lips. 'It's bit tender, but don't worry—I'm not contemplating litigation.'

'Probably wise in the circumstances,' he observed drily. 'The truth would do your career more harm than mine.'

'I wasn't doing anything wrong!' she protested.

'Ah, but someone in your position not only needs to be above suspicion, but to *appear* to be above suspicion.'

'That's a horribly cynical thing to say.'

'But true...'

'We'll have to agree to differ.' She accompanied her words with a tight smile that didn't reach her wary eyes. 'Don't worry yourself about my accommodation arrangements, but,' she added casually, as if the idea had just occurred to her, 'before I leave, I might as well take those photos and be out of your hair...' Some perverse mental process immediately made her visualise sliding her fingers deep into that dark, glossy thatch.

'I'm sure we can come to a mutually agreeable arrangement...'

'I don't want to be agreeable!' she bellowed, stamping her foot. There was absolutely no point playing it softly, softly with someone like him. 'I want the photos—*now!*'

Shock flickered across Javier's face. He was not accustomed to receiving peremptory orders from anyone, least of all from a slip of girl like this!

'*Dios Mio,* what a temper you have!' he exclaimed. 'Calm yourself. I'm sure we can negotiate something.'

'Negotiate?' she parroted, brushing a section of damp hair impatiently behind her ear.

Javier's nostrils flared as the clean scent of the shampoo she had just used drifted towards him, the scent subtly mingled with a warm female fragrance. He felt his body react to the stimulus. The strength of the response startled him.

'Negotiation...I want something, you want something, we come to a mutually beneficial arrangement, possibly involving an acceptable degree of compromise,' he elucidated slowly in his rich dark chocolate drawl. 'I would have thought as a lawyer you were au fait with the way it works.'

Now, *compromise* worried her, but the idea of him wanting something she had worried her a lot more!

'What do I have that you want?' Kate quavered, wrapping her arms protectively across her chest. Though the droop of his heavy lids concealed the expression in his eyes, she could detect a worrying gleam through the lush screen.

'I need to get married.'

It was not a response she had expected.

'Congratulations,' Kate responded uncertainly. Trained to observe such things, she automatically noted the slight emphasis on *need* and the significant absence of want, both verbally and non-verbally.

'You have not asked me in what manner this concerns you?'

'I thought you'd get around to telling me…*eventually,*' she observed with an exaggerated sigh.

Her response made his lips quirk appreciatively.

'My grandfather is an old-fashioned man in many ways…' he began heavily.

'This might be quicker if I tell you what I already know. You're talking about Felipe Montero. The one with money, power and grasping relations all jockeying for position to replace him?' The financial pages were not Kate's choice of reading but she'd have needed to be living in a vacuum if she hadn't known something of the circumstances.

'The one with terminal cancer,' came the blunt response.

Kate's scornful smirk drooped. 'Oh, God! I'm so sorry,' she murmured, feeling a total, thoughtless cow. 'I didn't know.'

'That is not accidental; nobody does. If the financial markets learn of his illness, the bottom will drop out of Montero shares, wiping millions off the company's value overnight. To the world, my grandfather *is* Montero,' he outlined unemotionally. 'The obvious solution is for the mantle to pass smoothly to his successor before it becomes public knowledge.'

The cold-bloodedness of this analysis appalled Kate. Searching his face gave her no insight into his attitude towards his grandfather's illness. Did it really mean no more to him than figures on a balance sheet? Was he really that callous?

'You want to be his successor.'

'I am the logical choice. My uncle and cousins, whilst all are capable in their own way, lack leadership qualities.'

Kate marvelled at his astonishing arrogance. 'But you

have those qualities…?' She couldn't tell if he'd recognised the irony in her tone as he calmly conceded her point.

'I do, and I see no reason to deny the fact. I would have thought that you of all people would appreciate candour, but I was forgetting the British consider self-deprecation a virtue,' he drawled. 'Does that make me an arrogant Spaniard?'

His mockery made Kate flush angrily. 'I don't see your problem. Your grandfather needs an heir—you are it. What does it have to do with me?'

'My grandfather and I have not always seen eye to eye; he is not a flexible man…'

This classic demonstration of the pot calling the kettle black brought a grim smile to her lips; as amusing as this was she couldn't see where she came into it. 'Will you get to the damned point?' she pleaded tautly.

'He had let me know that I am his choice but—this is where his old-fashioned standards come into it—only if I am married. He has even gone to the trouble of providing me with a potential mate.'

'Doesn't he think you can find one of your own?' The mocking smile faded dramatically from her face as an extraordinary explanation for his grandfather's intervention presented itself to her. *'You're not…?'* Kate gasped. Another look revealed a tall figure oozing a staggering amount of aggressive masculinity; she smiled a little at her own stupidity and shook her head—*no way* was his sexual orientation in question! There had to be another explanation, but what?

'Not what?' Javier puzzled impatiently.

Kate's eyes dropped from his as she shook her head, extremely relieved she'd managed to put a brake on her impetuous tongue in time to stop her looking a total idiot and probably mortally offending him in the bargain. There were certain things you didn't ask a male and that went double if he was a Spanish male! Questioning his masculinity definitely came into that category of questions and the last thing she needed was a swaggering display of testosterone.

An incredulous exclamation suddenly burst from Javier's lips as he watched the play of expression on her face. Without warning, he reached out and cupped her chin in his hand, raising her chin. Kate didn't offer any resistance, she was too startled to do anything but stare up at him.

For an intensely uncomfortable moment which, for Kate, seemed to last for an eternity he searched her face.

'*Madre mia!*' he breathed as an incredulous expression spread across his face. 'That *is* what you meant, isn't it?' he marvelled.

Guilty colour flooded Kate's cheeks as she jerked her chin from his light grasp and dropped down into a convenient chair her knees shaking uncontrollably.

'I might be able to confirm or deny if I had the faintest idea what you were talking about...' she prevaricated stiffly.

'My sexual orientation is not something I've been called upon to defend before,' he mused.

Kate covered her face and groaned. How could you argue with someone who appeared to possess the ability to read your mind?

'But,' he continued silkily, 'I've never been one to duck a challenge...' Kate peeked through her parted fingers; she didn't like the sound of that steely sentiment or the worrying gleam in his eyes. 'Let me reassure you I do *like* women. *Exclusively,*' he added grinning wolfishly.

And I bet they like you right back.

'I'm happy for you,' she choked. 'It was only a passing thought,' she added, trying to defuse the situation. 'No need for any rash demonstrations; I'm totally prepared to believe you're rampantly heterosexual.' The thought that any demonstration might take the form of something crude—like a kiss—made it hard for her not to hyperventilate.

It would naturally be horrifying and appalling to be kissed under these circumstances. Part of her couldn't help but wonder if the price wouldn't be worth paying, just to satisfy her curiosity... What would it feel like to be kissed by Javier Montero?

'That makes me feel a great deal easier.'

Kate's eyes narrowed as she glared at him with resentful dislike. 'But I soon realised you weren't gay, just too immature to contemplate commitment.' A person had a right to think stupid things without being called upon to defend her thoughts. 'For one daft moment there I was actually worried about your fragile Spanish male ego coping with a perceived slur on your manhood.'

'It was a close thing for a minute...' he conceded drily.

'A force ten hurricane couldn't dent your ego!' Kate snorted.

'I'm sorry if I fail to comply with your stereotyping of Southern Mediterranean man, Kate. I'll walk around with my shirt open to the waist.' He flicked open a button at mid-chest level and revealed a section of deep golden flesh covered with a light sprinkling of dark hair. He contemplated the area with a lot more composure than she did. 'And wear a flashy gold medallion, maybe.' His head lifted. 'What do you think?' he appealed to her with searing sarcasm. 'Will a little tacky exhibitionism make you feel more secure? Or shall I pinch your bottom?'

Secure? Kate, the blood pounding heavily in her temples, dragged her glazed eyes from the section of tanned skin. While she was in the same country as this infuriating man who twisted everything she said, she wouldn't feel secure.

'I do not stereotype people,' she denied hotly. 'It's just you *are* single and not exactly in the first flush of youth...' Even to Kate's ears, this sounded a pretty feeble excuse.

'Not that you're old exactly…' Way to go, Kate—call him gay and decrepit and he's bound to hand over the photos.

'So all unmarried men in their thirties are gay. Let me see, have I got this right?' he pondered innocently. 'That's *not* stereotyping?'

'I didn't mean anything of the sort!' Kate closed her eyes and sent up a silent prayer for deliverance. She took a steadying breath and met his eyes with what she hoped was some degree of composure. 'It's not as if I could give two hoots one way or the other where, when or with whom you have sex. It's your aversion to arranged marriages we were discussing… What's wrong, is your grandfather's choice of prospective bride the problem? Is she a bit of a dog?' She'd never thought to hear herself use such a derisory term to describe one of her own sex which just showed what a corrupting influence this man had upon her.

'No; as a matter of fact, Aria is beautiful and accomplished and in love with me…'

He seemed to accept this adulation in his stride; it must have something to do with having been on the receiving end of adulation all of his adult life, she supposed.

'How nice for you.'

'I do not love her.'

'And that matters to you?' She couldn't hide her scepticism.

Did men like him marry for love? It surprised Kate that he even knew the meaning of the word!

But then who am I to talk? It's not as if I'm the expert, she thought gloomily reviewing her love life—it took all of ten seconds! Seb had been the only serious boyfriend she'd ever had, her first lover and sometimes she thought maybe her last! Not that she was pining; once the dust had settled she'd realised the only part of her hurt by the experience was her pride.

Maybe Seb had had a point when he'd said there was no point staying in a relationship that was going nowhere.

'I'll always come second to your career,' he'd accused. Well it hadn't taken him long to find a girl who put him first; they were expecting their first baby any time now.

'But I am fond of Aria, too fond to marry her. So what I need is a woman who will go through a ceremony with me; after a suitable interval we would part.'

Kate stiffened; the pupils of his eyes dilated dramatically as she stared up at him—he couldn't be suggesting...? *Could he?* She gave a wry smile and shook her head. Maybe that knock on the head had fused a few circuits, because nobody with a full complement of wits could imagine even briefly he'd come up with a plan like that!

'I wouldn't have thought you'd have a lot of trouble finding someone to oblige you, especially if the remuneration for the contract is generous,' she observed cynically. Actually, she could think of several women who would do it for free!

Even she could see the more obvious attractions of such a scheme.

'My grandfather is a highly intelligent man. He would not be deceived by some plausible gold-digger.' The furrows across his broad brow deepened as he re-examined the problem. 'I need someone *different*...preferably British and fair... Someone who will not be easily intimidated... Someone who at the end of the day will go back to her own life and leave me to mine.'

'Why British and fair?' Kate asked, intrigued despite herself by the reference that stood out in a truly bizarre speech as more puzzling than the rest.

'Because he knows that the woman I fell in love with is both.' Kate gasped but Javier continued, 'You find the notion of me loving someone so incredible?'

Actually she found the fact of some woman having the

good sense not to love him back incredible because, whatever else he was, he had sex appeal oozing out of every pore.

'Nice dental work, Kate,' he observed dryly, 'but the open-mouthed look is not a good one for you.'

Kate closed her mouth with an audible snap.

'Why don't you marry this woman?'

'That was my plan, although I doubt if she realised it, but that's irrelevant. She fell in love with someone else, someone who happens to be one of my best friends.'

Surely this was a man who wouldn't be constrained by the limits of polite society? Failure of any sort must be unpalatable in the extreme to a man of his disposition. It didn't matter how hard she tried to picture Javier as a rejected suitor, she couldn't! Her eyes drifted to the sensual outline of his mouth...why, even I would be *slightly* tempted in the unlikely scenario of him making a pass at me and I don't even like dark brooding types.

'And that puts her off limits?' It brought him down to a worryingly human level to discover he'd actually experienced rejection.

'This has nothing to do with morals; you cannot make someone love you.'

Undeterred by the repressive chill in his voice, she was unable to restrain herself from pushing it. For some reason she found his pragmatism depressing. She might accept her own fate with similar stoicism but, although she might personally prefer her men predictable with manageable-sized passions, the closet romantic in her wanted there to be men out there with souls of fire and passion, men who would fight with his dying breath to win over the woman he loved!

'Did you try?'

An unreadable expression, that might have been his equivalent of a violent emotional outburst, flickered across his taut features. 'What is this, a counselling session?'

'I see you did, but she wouldn't. Wow! I'd really like to meet her!' she responded incautiously.

'You shall. Sarah has agreed to be a witness at our wedding tomorrow.'

CHAPTER SEVEN

KATE blinked several times and waited until the room appeared the right way up once more before hoarsely responding. 'Come again…'

'*Come again…?* I am not familiar with the term.'

'My eye! The ignorance card isn't going to get you off this hook, mate!' Kate exploded. 'You must be out of your tiny mind if you think I'm going to agree to marry you so you can inherit the family store!'

Javier coughed; it took him several moments to adjust to hearing a multi-billion empire dismissively referred to as the 'family store.' 'It will cause you the minimum of inconvenience—a paper arrangement, no more.'

He was clearly unbalanced. 'I hope this Aria of yours is no relation, because I'm getting the strong impression here that there's already been a bit too much in-breeding in your family. Cousins marrying cousins, that sort of thing, if you get my drift…?'

'I thought you wanted the photos.'

A pained expression of regret crossed Kate's face, but perhaps it was best this way; maybe it was time Susie started taking responsibility for her own actions.

'I care for my sister.' Her eloquent sniff managed to intimate that he didn't know the meaning of the word. 'I'd do a great deal for her…'

His eyes touched the bruised area on her temple. 'Most people would say you already have.'

'But marrying a blackmailing lunatic is not one of them.'

'My grandfather will really like your candour.'

Kate threw up her hands. What I really need to do, she

decided, is take a deep breath and stand back from all this *weirdness*. Far enough away, this situation might even have a funny side…?

'Are you not listening to me?' Silly question—of course he wasn't; he obviously didn't listen to anyone. 'I'm not going to marry you!' she delivered firmly, drawing a shaky hand threw her damp hair. 'Not even if you send those photos to the newspapers, but you might like to reflect when you do it that when it comes down to it you're no better than that scumbag who drugged my sister and took them!' Bosom heaving, lip curled in contempt, she met his eyes.

What she saw on his face made her catch her breath and hold it. Maybe she'd gone too far, she reflected, as he visibly fought to control the rage that contorted his lean features… She watched as inch by inch he gained control until only the throbbing pulse beside his mouth was left to remind her of that blaze of consuming fury.

'They're yours.'

Kate stared at the packet he placed on her lap suspiciously. 'Is this some sort of trick?'

'I am not interested in shaming a family because of the mistake of one member and, as for Gonzalez, he will not escape justice.'

From any other man, Kate might have taken this as an idle boast but when Javier said it there was nothing idle or boastful about it—he was just stating fact, and she found herself accepting it as such.

She picked up the buff envelope and found her fingers were trembling—there had to be a catch. 'Isn't this your bargaining chip in the negotiation we were talking about? It hardly makes sense for you to give it away.'

'I am a tough negotiator, not a petty criminal,' he replied, the pride that had remained unruffled by her clumsy attack on his masculinity clearly offended by her opinion of his business acumen.

'Then I don't understand...' A small scornful smile curved her lips. 'Oh, you probably think everyone has their price...! Yes,' she mused letting her glance move over him from head to toe and back again, 'you would.'

The dark fan of lashes lifted from his cheek; his expression radiated confidence. 'It's just a matter of discovering what it is.'

The sinister implication that he had found hers made Kate shiver. She dismissed the idea as foolish; she had many sins but avarice was not one of them.

'You shouldn't judge everyone else by your own standards. You see, I don't want your money...' she revealed, injecting a note of pity into her tone that brought a satisfactory flare of annoyance to his eyes.

'Not for yourself, perhaps...'

Kate frowned. 'What do you mean...?'

'I was thinking about the project to provide an extension on the burns unit at the children's hospital you yourself were treated at, and the new accommodation facilities in the existing unit so that families of patients having long-term treatment can stay with their children...'

Kate surged to her feet, her body rigid with suspicion. Though it might be important to her and others involved, their fund-raising activities on behalf of the unit barely rated a mention in the local press, let alone any journal he might have read. Unless she talked in her sleep, there was no way he could know about them.

'What do you know about that?' she demanded, hardly able to hear herself past the alarm bells clanging in her head. 'H-how did you find out...? Did my parents tell you or...?'

'I have not seen your parents since last night.'

'Then how?'

'The how is irrelevant.' He dismissed her questions with a fluid gesture.

Kate's full lips compressed. 'Not to me it isn't.' She raised a hand to her spinning head and tried to think straight.

'It's not complicated. Information is easy to find at any time of the day if you know where to look, and who to ask.'

And he clearly did. What was obvious normal practice for him appalled her. *Implacable,* the word flashed into Kate's head as she met his impassive stare with one of incredulity.

'It's easy to invade someone's privacy, you mean,' she corrected, her distaste for his questionable tactics written clearly across pale, outraged features as she lifted her eyes to his.

'Someone in my position knows only too well how easy,' he agreed heavily. 'One learns the hard way how to protect oneself from intrusions.'

His hypocrisy was staggering! 'Clearly you don't believe in the principle of treating others as you would be treated yourself,' she observed contemptuously. 'What other questions did you ask about me when you were grubbing around in my life?'

'Only relevant ones.'

On anyone else, Kate would have been inclined to believe the slight flush along his cheekbones might have been a reflection of discomfort. 'Such as?'

'I know that you have no lover who might be an obstacle to our plan.'

As her knees sagged, Kate's hand closed over the nearest thing to hand, which happened to be Javier's forearm; it immediately stiffened to offer her extra support.

'*Our* plan…? *Your* plan!' she contradicted, wanting to disassociate herself with this absurd scheme straight off.

She stared at the image of her white-knuckled fingers digging into crisp cotton; she stared so hard everything else swam out of focus. Underneath the thin material she was conscious of the crisp texture of fine body hair, the heat of his skin and overlying everything else the sinewy iron strength. The stab of sexual energy that sizzled through her body was so unexpected, so shockingly intense, it took her breath away. Kate removed her hand as if burnt as her stomach took a great diving lurch downwards.

Head bent, hands braced on her thighs, she exhaled in a series of short panting breaths before she dared to lift her eyes to his. It was mortifying to discover she was so sexually receptive to someone she despised so completely, someone to whom she was no more than a tool to be callously manipulated for his own financial gain.

When she did angle a wary glance up at him, she was dismayed to see a flicker of something perilously close to sympathy in his eyes. That look seemed to say he understood her reactions better than she did herself. Not that that would be so damned hard, because at that moment Kate had never had less insight into what she was feeling or why!

Determined that, if nothing else, she would at least show him she was not another silly female who swooned at the sight of him, she returned the look with one of smouldering derision.

'What would you have done if I had had a boyfriend, Javier, arranged for him to have an *accident?*' she asked sarcastically. Her glance slid over his tall figure and hard, ruthless features and suddenly it didn't seem such a joke any more—he looked capable of *anything*.

'Now you are being hysterical,' he observed, his attitude that of someone getting bored with the entire discussion.

Kate gave a disbelieving laugh—was he for real…? 'No, but I'm getting there,' she told him grimly. 'And your in-

formation is wrong. I do have a boyfriend, Seb Leigh…'
She served a smug little smile. 'He's a QC and he's—'

'I'm sure his CV is as impressive as your own,' came
the cool contradiction. 'However, Mr Leigh *was* your lover,
isn't that so, Kate? Your second serious relationship, I believe…?' He appeared to interpret the choking sound that
emerged from Kate's throat as confirmation of this. 'But he
is out of the picture. You split up a year ago and he is now
married to someone else. Does that bother you?'

Kate stood there seething and feeling as foolish as anyone would caught pretending to have a relationship. What
made her angriest was the impression it gave that she felt
somehow inadequate and incomplete without a man, when
nothing could have been farther from the truth.

'You mean your sources didn't supply you with that information? How annoying.'

'It is not actually relevant,' he conceded. 'I was just wondering if you have any regrets… Of course, many women
like yourself delay marriage, concentrating their energies
on building their career, not a family.'

'I intend to have both one day.'

'Unlike many career-minded women you seem to have
retained an oddly naïve quality,' he observed thoughtfully.

'What's so naïve about thinking you can have both?' she
began aggressively.

Javier acted as though she hadn't spoken. 'It is not unattractive,' he revealed in his rough velvet drawl.

He held her startled gaze for long enough to see her
shock register on her face before allowing his gaze to drop.

This unexpected development ambushed Kate's wits. Her
pulses went haywire; she went hot, she went cold; for several seconds the only thing she could do was tremble and
admire the luxuriant sweep of his lashes as they brushed
against his high cheekbones.

And why? she asked herself.

Just because he's deigned to say you're not totally repulsive! How sad it is that? A bit of mild ego-boosting and you start thinking with your hormones, which can't be a bad thing from his point of view; someone smitten with lust is going to be a lot more pliable. The last thing she wanted to do was make Javier Montero's life easier!

'But not your type, obviously…' If an insult was pending, Kate made it her rule to get in first.

The iridescent blue gaze landed back on her face and stayed there.

Kate suffered a second searing jolt in as many minutes.

Being a sensible woman meant that she didn't read anything personal in the smouldering intensity she encountered when their eyes locked. Sensuality was innate to him; it was revealed in his slightest movement, the proud angle of his head, his voice… Another shiver snaked on her spine at the thought of his honeyed, husky drawl.

Her body either couldn't or didn't want to hear what she was telling it, because it responded brazenly to the glitter in his spectacular eyes. As she struggled to control the violent fluctuations of her breathing, she was acutely conscious of the burning sensitivity in her engorged nipples and the ache low in her belly.

'I wouldn't contemplate marrying anyone I found repulsive,' he revealed.

'Neither would I,' she retorted instantly. '*Normally*. What's so funny?' she demanded.

'You are a very bad liar.'

'No, I'm not!' she retorted indignantly. Amusement flared afresh in his eyes and Kate bit her lip. 'That is, I'm not lying.'

For what seemed like a long time he surveyed her with that air of inscrutable calm she found so exasperating; finally he shrugged. 'If you prefer for your own reasons to pretend you are totally unaware of the sexual chemistry that exists between us, I will naturally accept your wishes. These causes you espouse,' he continued seamlessly. 'They do require funds?'

There was a twenty-second time lag before his words made much sense to Kate, who had a lot more trouble than he appeared to have in shifting her turbulent thoughts from personal to business.

'We are raising money. The raft race, the sponsored—' she began numbly.

Sexual chemistry, he'd said. She swallowed hard as her eyes darted furtively towards his mouth. Oh, hell, Kate why did you deny it, act as if it was some big deal? Why didn't you just shrug it off? Maybe because you knew you couldn't?

He clicked his fingers. 'A drop in the ocean,' he responded dismissively.

'We'll get there.' Of course, an awful lot of sick kids would have grown up by then—the lucky ones anyway.

'You'll get there a lot faster if I make up the shortfall,' he interrupted casually.

Kate laughed shakily. 'Have you any idea how much that is? We're not talking hundreds or even thousands, we're talking—'

'Millions—yes, I know,' he interrupted calmly.

Kate's jaw dropped. 'And you'll pay for that?' She gulped—this man had taken moral blackmail to another level! What he was offering would mean so much to so many people. The injured children, the parents, the highly trained team of staff whose hard work and dedication could only partly compensate for a chronic lack of investment in the burns unit. How will I feel the next time a child is turned away because there is no spare bed, if I know that I could have made the difference...?

'If you agree to marry me I'll sign the cheque now... You fill in the amount.' He watched, arms folded across his chest, as the conflicting emotions tripped across her face.

Kate couldn't take her eyes from the cheque and pen he placed on the table. She touched her tongue to the beads of sweat across her upper lip.

'This money doesn't mean anything to you, does it? The children it could help, they mean nothing to you either? No more than I do?' He responded to her whispered accusation with a shrug—what did you expect? Him to dramatically reveal it's really you he wants, not control of the Montero empire?

Her trembling lips compressed into a mutinous line. 'What if I say I will, then I bank the money and back out at the last minute?' she asked, licking her dry lips.

His smiled thinly. 'I trust you, you are a woman of principle…' He made it sound like a vice. 'One who will put the welfare of others ahead of her own personal desires…'

Kate lifted her eyes an expression of loathing on her face. 'I'm not a martyr.'

'No,' he conceded. 'A martyr would marry me to save her family embarrassment. You will marry me to help thousands of children have better care in the future, because you care passionately about them.'

'Are you so sure of me?' she wondered, trying to hide her growing sense of despair.

'Yes, I am. We can argue for a while if you like—but your decision is inevitable and we both know it.'

Kate swallowed convulsively. 'I have a career.'

'I'm not asking you to give it up; a short sabbatical should suffice for our purposes.'

'I'll want everything in writing and you'll give the money to the unit up front?' I'm mad, quite mad…

'Naturally.'

'Including a clause that guarantees you don't lay a finger on me?'

'You can't legislate against passion between two people.' His glance moved over her body in a way that made her aware of it all over again in a very disturbing way. 'Will my word not suffice?'

Kate threw back her head and laughed to hide the fact she was still seriously spooked by his reference to passion. 'That's the funniest thing I've ever heard. I wouldn't take your word for it if you told me the sun is going to rise tomorrow.'

There was real loathing in her eyes as she glared up at him; Javier regretted her animosity but felt it was a small price to pay for letting his grandfather die a happy man— it was a pity, though. In other circumstances he suspected they could have been friends... Well, maybe not friends, not with the lust factor.

'And they say trust is the most important thing in a marriage,' he sighed.

CHAPTER EIGHT

JAVIER was sitting tapping his index finger impatiently against the steering wheel when the fair-headed figure finally appeared around the corner. As he watched she gave a quick furtive glance over one shoulder, then the other.

He half expected her to daub her face with camouflage paint and slither across the courtyard on her belly, commando-style, but as he watched she lifted her rounded little chin and took a deep breath; then, shoulders back walked purposefully towards the car as fast as the pair of ridiculously high-heeled strappy sandals she wore would allow. Clearly she was too proud to allow him to see her apprehension, Javier concluded with grudging admiration.

As Kate approached the long shiny car, the tinted window on the driver's side lowered. A supremely confident Javier, his lean body clad in a dark formal suit, was revealed at the wheel. Sometimes the drivers of classy cars were a bit of a let-down, but not in this case!

Kate stopped dead in her tracks as he slowly lowered the stylish dark shades he wore and looked at her over the top. She felt every muscle in her body grow tense and rigid as she endured his laser like scrutiny.

Elbow resting on the open window, his long fingers drummed against the shiny paintwork as he waited expectantly. 'Don't just stand there, get in!'

Kate flushed at the peremptory tone. 'I was just trying to decide whether what I'm doing could be termed elopement,' she replied, in an attempt to divert attention from the embarrassing fact she'd been staring at him with all the subtlety of a star-struck adolescent!

'Or if it's only elopement when star-crossed lovers are involved?' she finished, panting slightly as she took her place beside him in the passenger seat.

The mild exertion Javier noted had brought a very attractive flush to the smooth contours of her cheeks; he couldn't place the perfume but she also smelt rather good.

'You are late!' he rapped.

Kate, who had been about to apologise for her tardiness, closed her mouth with a snap. The sudden eye movement as she dealt him a cold look made her conscious of the irritating presence of the contact lenses she rarely wore—damned things.

'I had a visit from Susie; I had to wait until she'd gone, or would you prefer I'd brought her along…?'

She pushed a hank of fair hair from her face with her forearm and wondered if perhaps it might not have been better to put it up after all. Until Susie's comment about the length of her neck—there was too much of it, apparently—she had thought the loose chignon was not only cool but quite attractive.

Kate had been rather touched by Susie's unexpected visit to her sick bed until she realised that her sister had come to make sure that she had managed to retrieve the negatives before she'd been taken ill. Susie had been extremely relieved when Kate had handed over the envelope.

Once her own problems were solved, an elated Susie had moved on to the next thing on her agenda—Javier Montero and how did well Kate know him anyhow?

It had been insultingly easy for Kate to convince her sister that her own supposed friendship with the fabled Javier Montero was a big misunderstanding.

'I knew it was,' Susie had revealed smugly. 'I mean, no insult intended, Katie, but the likes of Javier Montero is hardly likely to date someone like you.' But not someone like me, her smug expression seemed to imply.

'True, but that's his loss,' Kate had replied grandly.

'That's right, Katie.' Susie patted her sister's shoulder in an encouraging manner. 'I do so admire your positive attitude. Tell me,' she added casually, 'is he seeing anyone at the moment?'

'Positive attitude nothing! If I had that man for a couple of weeks I might be able to teach him a bit of humility,' Kate boasted ambitiously. 'And that,' she declared, 'would be doing womankind a big favour!'

'But, Kate, when I saw him he was charming!'

'If you were wearing that outfit, I'm not surprised!' Kate retorted; the idea of Javier slobbering over her nubile baby sister was particularly unappealing.

Susie laughed and slid her hands complacently over her slim, evenly tanned hips.

'Stay away from him, Susie!' Kate advised abruptly.

Susie stared at her in astonishment.

'He'd eat you up and spit you out. He's a devious snake,' Kate had elaborated with so much vehemence that her sister had laughed nervously and remembered a previous engagement.

Just how she was going to explain away her comments when Susie discovered she'd married the snake she didn't know, but when she considered her other problems this one didn't rate priority treatment! No matter what spin you put on it, the bottom line was Javier had bought his bride, and she was it!

Despite her initial reluctance to keep her family in the dark, the encounter with Susie had made her think that Javier had a point when he had said that the fewer people that knew about this beforehand the better. There was certainly no way she was going to convince anyone who knew her that she was anything other than a very reluctant bride!

Javier gave her a veiled look. 'You would have preferred the support of your family today...?'

Rebellion simmering not far below the surface flared up as she eyed him resentfully.

'Hardly!' she responded scornfully. 'Marrying you is not an event I'd want anyone I know to witness; I've got a reputation as a rational human being to protect. Or did you mean it in a someone to hold while you're having a tooth pulled sort of way? Or maybe…'

The sound of his hissing exhalation brought her diatribe to an abrupt halt. She got the impression that he wanted to say quite a lot to her but he contented himself with, 'I'm prepared to put up with your sarcasm up to a point.'

Despite his level tone Kate was left with the impression that dismissal was implicit in his cool manner. Kate, who had felt nervous and anxious when she'd got into the car, felt her anger climb. She watched as he loosened a button of his exquisitely cut jacket before adjusting the driving mirror a fraction; it was obvious to her that he was a man to whom such minor details were important. He was also a man who she knew next to nothing about… So far, she'd kept her anxiety levels in check by not thinking too far ahead, but she wouldn't have that luxury soon, she'd be married!

Filled by pure panic, she launched immediately into a vitriolic attack.

'If you want people to believe this marriage is for real, you'll have to start talking to me as if I'm a human being, not a disobedient puppy being brought to heel…' Yes, mate, she thought as he turned his head, I can actually instigate a conversation without permission.

For a split second she thought he was going to explode, then a dangerous, contemplative expression slid across his grim features. She observed the transformation with deep foreboding.

'In what sense, *real?'*

Kate's head snapped back at this totally unexpected response. Heat flooded her face; the speculative gleam in his eyes made it impossible for her to mistake his meaning.

'Not that one!' she advised him darkly.

Aware his glance had wandered to her legs, neatly crossed at the ankle, she began smoothing down the skirt of her short cream shift dress, angry at herself for allowing him to discompose her so easily.

Her actions drew his gaze and inevitably his criticism—the girl he married for real was in for a rough ride, she decided sourly.

'You are wearing *that?*' If he were to be her husband in the real sense, the idea of other men lustfully ogling those long, extremely shapely legs would have disturbed him.

Kate drew herself up huffily. She may have to marry him; she wasn't going to let him criticise her dress sense into the bargain! Even if the dress in question had returned from the dry cleaners a good two inches shorter than it went there... This discovery had almost reduced her to tears, but there had been no time to change.

'I had this boyfriend once,' she explained, as she fixed him with a dangerously narrowed gaze. 'He thought I ought to wear winter colours, whatever they might be. He also wanted me to grow my hair and shorten my skirts... I have to tell you he lasted about five minutes, but I expect you've already learnt this from your in-depth dossier on my life and loves...' she observed sweetly.

'Your love life didn't take up much space, which surprises me for you are clearly a very sensual, passionate woman.' This frank observation was accompanied by a slow, sensual smile of the heart-stopping variety.

Kate felt her composure, already in pretty bad shape from sharing a confined space with him, shatter into a thousand fragments.

'Leave my love life out of this!'

'But you introduced the subject.'

'I wasn't introducing any subject; I was simply laying down a few ground rules,' Kate gritted.

'*You,* are laying down rules for *me!*' he responded with an air of startled incredulity.

Kate shrugged. 'You can like it or lump it.'

His eyes narrowed. 'I thought me *not* liking it was what this was about; you are determined to make the time we spend together as unpleasant as possible. Do you always feel the need to be in charge in a relationship?'

'We don't have a relationship.'

'Not of the conventional kind,' he conceded.

'Not of any kind.'

'We're going to be seeing quite a lot of one another, and life would be a lot more comfortable if rather than pick fights you tried to get along with me...'

'That's a big ask.'

'If you're nourishing some hope that I will find you so intolerable I will call off the wedding—don't. Incidentally, did the hospital receive the funds...?'

'Yes.' His smooth question threw her off balance.

David Fenner, the clinical director, had been euphoric. 'I don't know how to thank you,' he kept saying over and over. 'Please tell the anonymous donor how much this means to us, Kate. It's a marvellous thing he's doing for us.' It was at that moment Kate had realised that she'd burnt her boats big time!

'They were grateful.'

'I don't want their gratitude.' She felt him studying her face and lifted her head. 'I want you.'

Kate knew he didn't mean it that way, but all the same she felt the knot of sexual heat in her belly swell to bursting point. 'I have that effect on men.'

Her quip didn't make him laugh the way it was meant to. If anything, the tension between them increased.

'I won't have you dictate what I wear,' she heard herself

babble. 'I'm sorry I don't meet your high standards...' Her glare moved disparagingly over his tastefully clad figure— nothing to criticise there; everything about him shrieked good taste and money. 'Though some people might consider your orthodox style a bit on the well...on the *insipid* side,' she mused spitefully. 'But then I suppose not everyone has an individuality to reflect...' Her spite suddenly ran out of steam as a giant wave of despondency hit her. 'Oh, God!' she groaned. 'I wish I'd just worn the pink shorts suit and been done with it.' That childish act of rebellion would have at least shown him how totally unsuitable she was for the role he wanted her to play.

'And I'm sure you'd have looked charming in it,' he responded grimly.

A sudden giggle welled in Kate's throat; the sound as it escaped made him stare at her in a startled fashion. 'You wouldn't have said that if you'd seen me in it. My bottom looked like the size of a double-decker bus...' she elaborated.

A gleam of startled amusement appeared in his eyes. 'You are very frank and rather severe on yourself. I didn't actually say that I didn't like your dress...' he reminded her, his eyes sliding of their own volition to her legs.

Kate viewed this blatant attempt to steer the conversation away from the thorny subject of her bottom with a sour smile. Of course, if he'd been a total hypocrite he could simply have said, *It's a delicious bottom, just the right size,* but Kate recognised this was not the most likely of scenarios!

'I couldn't care less!' she sniffed childishly.

'Then why are you making such an issue of it? The fact is, I have no desire to act as some sort of fashion police. I was merely vexed that I hadn't taken into account the likelihood you would not have a suitable outfit with you. I know women care about such things as wedding outfits...'

'Your concern is touching, but quite unnecessary. You're confusing me with a real blushing bride again. I'm not going to be flicking through the wedding album all dewy-eyed and remembering how fantastic you looked in your wedding suit—at least one of us looks the part,' she inserted bitterly.

'My appearance seems to bother you.'

'Everything about you bothers me!' she countered with a frustrated groan. 'Listen, there's no point acting as if this is a society wedding.' Kate was horrified to hear the wistful note in her voice…which, considering she had never lusted after a big wedding and all the frills in her life, had no right to be there in the first place! It was too much to hope he hadn't detected it too?

'You are angry because I have cheated you out of your opportunity to float down the aisle in white on your father's arm.'

'I'm not bitter, and as far as I'm concerned the fewer things I have to remind me of today the better, so you see the fact that I can bin this dress is no bad thing.'

Javier was just about to deliver a biting response to this sneering retort when he saw a single tear slip down her cheek. As he watched she brushed it away with the back of her hand and blinked rapidly to prevent any more escaping.

'I expect Sarah will have something you can wear over your head. That will have to suffice.'

The mention of the other woman made Kate glance across at him; it was impossible to tell from his expression what he felt when he said her name, or even if he felt anything!

'My manner was a little terse when you arrived because I do not like to be kept waiting…' This conciliatory tack made Kate wary. 'I think it's quite useful for you to know little details like this; it builds up a picture of familiarity…intimacy.'

'*Intimacy…!*' She laughed, her scorn more fierce because the mental link of intimacy and Javier stirred up an unsettling mess of confusing feelings deep in her stomach. 'If you think I'm ever going to be able to act cosy with you, you're a deeply deluded man,' she observed pityingly.

'But you will try…' he replied, with a hint of steel in his voice.

'It was part of the agreement,' she conceded uneasily.

'Just so long as you don't forget it…'

'Don't you dare threaten or…'

'Or what…?' Javier immediately regretted that he'd allowed her to goad him into this taunt.

Kate felt her temper rise. They both knew the answer; she could do nothing. Flushing darkly she looked away.

'And while we're talking manners I think your own might need a little modification also…?' he suggested drily as he turned the ignition.

'What's wrong with my manner?'

'You are petulant, confrontational and cranky,' he enumerated calmly.

'Well, that's one of those *little details* you should know about me. I'm always *cranky* when I'm being coerced into marrying a loathsome man I deeply despise. A man who will stoop to any depths in his pathetic pursuit of power and money—'

'Enough!' Javier's savage exclamation sliced through her furious diatribe. '*Madre mia,*' he snarled, his air of faint indulgence vanishing as his patience snapped. 'You will not speak to me in that manner.'

'*Really!* I thought it helped build up a picture of intimacy?' she returned innocently.

'*Por Dios!*' he breathed.

Kate felt the beginning of a guilty backlash to her nastiness as she watched him lean back in his seat. Pressing his head into the head rest, he closed his eyes and, with an expression of frustration on his face, dragged a hand through his dark hair.

She sighed as her sense of fair play kicked in hard... You'll probably regret this, she told herself as she cleared her throat. 'I'm sorry.'

He looked up, startled, at the soft apology.

'I'm not being fair. I didn't have to agree to marry you...it was my decision.' She sniffed and searched for a non-existent tissue. 'Thank you,' she murmured as a freshly laundered handkerchief was pressed into her sweaty palm. 'You dangled a carrot and I went for it...' So, as nice as it was to blame him for everything and absolve herself from all responsibility, it just wasn't on.

'I exploited your weakness.' An expression she didn't understand flickered into his iridescent eyes as they swept over her face. 'If caring about other people is a weakness?' he added softly.

'You get something you want and I get something I want.' Quietly she outlined the bare bones of their contract. 'You've kept your end of the bargain, I'll keep mine,' she promised with a stoic little grimace. 'I just think you could have invested your money more wisely.' Just thinking about the sheer volume of money they were talking scared her; for that amount he could have employed an Oscar-winning actress! 'Nobody is going to believe you wanted to marry *me*.'

'That is because...?'

'I'm not exactly a supermodel...'

'Is this any supermodel in particular or...?'

Kate bristled at his smooth sarcastic tone. 'You know what I mean.'

'I do indeed,' he replied, fingering the leather steering wheel.

Kate eyed his steel-reinforced jaw with some misgivings; it seemed even when she went out of the way to avoid conflict she still managed to aggravate him.

'I have to tell you again that I don't consider the British habit of self-deprecation an attractive one... Neither do I care for someone assuming to know what I find attractive in a woman.'

This was too much for Kate, who laughed in disbelief...he was different from other men, but she refused to believe he was *that* different.

'It's not exactly a *big* assumption. I'd say that ninety-nine point nine per cent of men in the world fantasise about women like that. The only difference between you and them—' other than a perfect masculine physique, a strikingly handsome face made to haunt a girl's dreams, and an indecent quantity of rampant sex appeal '—is you're in a position to do something about it,' she finished breathlessly—her unwise contemplation of what he had going for him had played havoc with her breathing.

Her wariness increased as Javier absorbed her words in brooding silence.

'My money, you mean.'

'Well, that too,' she conceded dismissively. She was sure that even had he been dirt-poor Javier would never have lacked female attention. 'But it was thinking more about your...' Kate stopped, aghast at what she'd been about to say. You couldn't go around telling men they were incredibly beautiful.

'My...?' he prompted attentively as her cheeks grew pink.

Kate gave a sigh of defeat. 'Well, it's not as if you're exactly bad to look at, are you?' she observed crossly. 'And don't act as if you didn't know.'

'I'm flattered, Kate...'

His blue-eyed mockery was just too much.

'No you're not, you're…' Javier watched as she valiantly struggled to bite back a scathing retort. 'I'm trying,' she gritted. 'I'm *really* trying, but it's really hard to be pleasant to you. I was just attempting…I know you're rich, but even for you we're not talking small change here. I'm just worried I'm not going to be good value for money,' Kate observed before she subsided into red-cheeked silence.

'Actually, I consider you excellent value for money,' he revealed in a tone that made his exact meaning hard to define. 'And leave me to worry about my money. I'm considered by some to be quite astute, financially speaking. Incidentally, though I appreciate your restraint, Kate, on the whole I think I prefer your acid retorts to the wooden dummy look.'

She was so relieved to be given the green light to speak her mind that she was prepared to overlook this unflattering comparison.

'Don't you think it's possible that the thought of losing your inheritance has affected your judgement…?' she began tentatively.

Maybe she was right, though not in the way she thought. Perhaps wanting to make his grandfather happy had blinded him to the inherent flaws in his scheme? He was certainly acting more on instinct than objectivity, but that didn't bother him too much. Javier believed strongly in following his gut instincts.

'Even if that were so, I'd hardly admit it, would I?'

'You wouldn't…?'

'Are you forgetting you're talking to an arrogant, conceited Spanish male? We are never wrong,' he explained with an ironic glint in his eyes. 'If you remember that in future, we'll deal very well together.'

This particular Spanish male was disturbingly attractive when he revealed that under his macho exterior there lurked an unexpectedly dry sense of humour.

'Thanks for the tip,' she responded in a similarly ironic vein. 'Any more on offer?'

'Well, treating my every pronouncement as though it is a pearl of wisdom would probably not come amiss,' he admitted gravely. 'And laugh at my jokes.'

Kate couldn't repress the gurgle of responsive laughter that bubbled up.

Not a man she'd thought to be easily disconcerted, Javier appeared so now. 'You have the *most* remarkable laugh!' he breathed.

Their eyes meshed, Kate stopped laughing, his held a searching quality that threw her into total confusion.

She began to clumsily struggle with her seat belt. Her efforts were futile; her co-ordination seemed to be in an advanced state of decay!

The engine was almost silent but when Javier switched it off she noticed. Well, she hadn't actually seen him do so, but it seemed safe to assume this had happened; this wasn't the sort of vehicle that conked out or stalled.

'What's wrong? You know, I think there's something wrong with this seat-belt...' she observed, tinkering with the clip.

He brought his hands down with a thud on the steering column. 'You are right,' he observed, turning to face her.

'Now there's something I never expected to hear you say,' she observed drily.

'We do not give the appearance of two people who have intimate knowledge of each other,' he pronounced flatly.

Kate's expression brightened. Could it be he was finally seeing that this ridiculous charade was doomed to failure? Once she recognised the flip side to this scenario, her hopeful expression faded. If he changed his mind about marriage she'd have to hand back the money, and she couldn't do that—not now, when they were already planning how to spend it! Perhaps she'd presented her arguments for the prosecution a little *too* successfully.

'You shy away from me when I touch you.'

Kate's plan had been not to look at him but the magnetic pull of his eyes proved greater than her willpower. 'That's because I don't like you touching me. I do *not!*' she added fiercely, in the face of his glittering scepticism. 'But,' she added, taking a deep breath, 'I expect I could get used to it.' An occasional hug and a bit of hand-holding was not a big price to pay for what he had given in return.

'That's extraordinarily generous of you.'

'The least I can do...'

'It's traditional for the groom to kiss the bride, Kate...' As he spoke his smoky eyes lingered suggestively on her mouth.

Kate was ashamed of the small bleating sound that emerged from her lips. 'If you're thinking of kissing me...?' she mumbled apprehensively.

It came as something of a shock to Javier to realise how much he'd been thinking about it, almost since the first moment he'd laid eyes on her. Now, of course, he had a perfectly legitimate reason to do so.

'There's something...'

'You should warn me about...?' he suggested helpfully.

Kate frowned at this frivolous interruption—what was Javier doing being frivolous, anyhow...? 'I've forgotten what I was going to say now!'

'Then don't say anything,' he suggested.

Kate's nervous system simply closed down as he took her face between his hands and drew her towards him.

Her eyes half closed as she swayed towards him. This wasn't the body language of rejection and Kate was painfully aware of the fact, but she felt curiously unwilling to do anything to correct the false impression she was giving.

This close to his masculinity was totally overwhelming.

Breathing in his male scent reminded her of the time she'd downed two glasses of champagne in quick succession at Seb's wedding reception, only this time she was *much* dizzier.

Shock, a knowledgeable voice in her head observed.

'No...!' Kate began, recovering control of her voice but little else.

She felt the feather-light touch of his fingertips sliding across her jaw and shivered. His burning gaze watched her soft, succulent lips as they parted slightly beneath the gentle pressure of his thumbs.

If you don't say something he will kiss you, the voice in her head warned—he might even think you want to. He might even be right!

There eyes met and Kate's insides seemed to melt. His olive skin was pulled taut over his slashing cheekbones and his masterful nose was covered by the faintest sheen of sweat. His warm breath, coming almost as fast as her own, fanned out over her cheek as their noses almost grazed. Kate half closed her eyes and inhaled the scent of his warm male body like an addict.

'You can tell a lot about a person from the way they kiss,' he explained thickly.

This didn't sound very scientific to Kate. 'A kiss is a kiss,' she protested huskily.

'Kissing also requires split-second timing,' he contradicted confidently.

'I knew that...' she whispered as he nipped gently at her full lower lip—could that be classified as a kiss? she puzzled as his fingers began to stroke her throat in light, feathery motions.

'It's extremely risky to let our first kiss be a public one—at the altar, even.'

He had a valid point. 'I hadn't thought of that.'

'These things need thinking about.'

His dark head lowered and her treacherous senses went wild in anticipation. His mouth covered hers, and there was nothing hard or invasive about the pressure as he kissed her gently.

Anticlimax.

Kate was dismayed to discover the almost chaste, teasing salute left her feeling cheated.

'That wasn't too bad,' she admitted hoarsely as his mouth lifted fractionally from hers. She prayed that none of her irrational pique showed in her face.

They were still so close she could see the individual gold flecks in the drowning sapphire of his eyes. Her breath snagged painfully in her throat as she witnessed his pupils dilating until the drowning blue was almost swallowed up by the inky blackness.

'A little bit of bad can be quite good,' he promised in a sexy rasp that made goose bumps break out all over her hot skin, just before he reasserted his authority over her mouth.

This time there was nothing even vaguely chaste about the deep, probing kiss. The erotic stabbing incursions of his tongue made her moan and wind her arms around his neck.

Later, she would try and convince herself that this had been a calculated—callous, even—attack on her senses, by a man who'd been the centre of female attention since he could smile, but at that moment nothing much mattered but the wave after incredible wave of scalding sensation that washed over her as he sank deeper into the warm recesses of her mouth.

When he lifted his mouth from hers, Kate's fingers were tangled in the dark hair on his nape and she was panting frantically. It was several sweaty seconds before she could prise her eyelids, which felt as though they were weighed down with lead, apart.

The combustible heat from his blue-eyed gaze, besides

making the sensitive muscles of her stomach cramp viciously alerted her to the way her body was pressed closely to his virile torso—second skin wouldn't have been pressing the point!

She drew back with a sharp gasp and fell back, her head against the padded restraint as she panted for Britain. She was vaguely aware that his actions had roughly followed the same pattern.

Almost in unison they turned their heads. Where Kate had expected smugness, perhaps a hint of gloating, she saw a look that on anyone else she'd have described as disconcerted.

'Good practice session,' she managed, between gasps. 'But quite honestly I don't think you need it.'

Credit where credit was due. Whatever else Javier Montero was he was a quite spectacularly good kisser—this didn't automatically mean he was a spectacular lover too, but the odds were definitely stacked in his favour!

Not that she was ever likely to put the theory to the test.

His eyes dropped to her lush lips. 'Neither do you.'

Kate shifted in her seat; perhaps some explanation for her enthusiastic response was called for. Obviously this was what happened when you became a slave to your work and ignored your more *basic* needs. She could hardly tell him this without making herself sound like a sad, sexually deprived loser.

'Well, I think we might be able to muddle through at the ceremony now,' she heard herself claim brightly.

'I think a modified version might be appropriate for that occasion.'

Dots of feverish colour appeared on her smooth cheeks. 'I think I might be able to restrain myself from ripping off your clothes.' Though it won't be easy, she thought, averting her covetous gaze from his arresting profile. 'About the wedding…' she began tentatively.

'You are nervous?'

'Would that be so surprising?' she charged, resenting his careless attitude. 'I've never been married before, and I'm not as practised at deception as you obviously are. I'd feel slightly more comfortable…if that is the right word,' she mused wryly, 'if there weren't too many surprises.'

'There will be no surprises, just the padre and Sarah and her husband as witnesses.'

'What's Sarah like?' Kate blushed as the impetuous words escaped, but rather to her surprise he didn't comment on her tasteless display of curiosity.

'She is gentle and sweet, and not nearly as robust, emotionally speaking, as you.'

Kate was less than flattered to discover that he clearly thought of her as some emotional Amazon.

She gritted her teeth. 'Sensitive qualities can be such a handicap.' Not that he was ever likely to suffer on that count, he had the sensitivity of a brick.

'I have offended you.'

'Not in the least, we emotionally robust types are by definition pretty tough.'

'It was not intended as an insult, quite the opposite. You are resourceful and independent; not all women have your confidence and natural resources. Sarah is a…*fragile* person, who is less well equipped than yourself to cope with the demands of modern life.'

'You mean if you'd accused her of being in cahoots with some sleazy drug-dealer she'd—'

'There was no way I would have made that mistake…' Javier interposed quickly.

'I should recognise her straight off, then; she's the one *without* the natural criminal tendencies I exude.'

'There is no need to be facetious.'

Kate, who thought there was every need, maintained a restrained silence.

'I met Sarah when my sister was in a drug rehabilitation programme in England; she was a fellow patient being treated for an eating disorder.'

Kate's cynical expression faded, as did her detachment; despite his opinion she had a soft, vulnerable heart. 'Your sister was…?'

'Addicted to drugs. Yes, she was.' Despite his remote expression, Kate could sense that his sister's dependence had deeply affected him. She took him to be the type of man who shouldered the mantle of responsibility for all those close to him. Kate sighed; his sister's sad history explained away the puzzle of his personal involvement when he had discovered someone was dealing drugs at the hotel.

'She became friends with Sarah during their stay and late that year my sister invited her to join us on the island.'

'And you fell in love with her?'

He stiffened. 'That was something I mentioned in confidence…'

'As if I'm going to blab about it.'

'I've offended you again.' He seemed intrigued by this discovery.

'Forget it; it's like water off a duck's back with us emotionally robust types. You're not hoping to make this Sarah of yours jealous with me, are you?'

'She is not my Sarah,' he retorted with frigid disapproval.

'Fair enough. Your sister, is she all right now…?'

Javier searched her face and instead of the prurient curiosity he'd expected he discovered a genuine concern. 'Thank you, yes, she is. She is studying modern history at Oxford.'

Kate beamed with disingenuous pleasure.

'That's good. You know,' she told him, reaching across and squeezing his hand lightly, 'you shouldn't blame yourself. These thing happen. The important thing is you were there for your sister when she needed you.' Seeing the direction of his disconcerted gaze, Kate removed her hand and, blushing deeply, sat on it.

'How do you know I was there for her?' With an expression she found impossible to interpret, his interest focused on her hot face.

'Well, I just assumed...' She stopped and gave an exasperated sigh—what was the point in beating about the bush? 'Well, if you must know,' she informed him frankly, 'you come across as the sort of person who would be there...' This admission surprised her as much as it seemed to him. 'But then,' she admitted with a wry grin, 'I always was a terrible judge of character!'

There was a short, tense silence before he began to smile, the transformation of his grim features was nothing short of miraculous.

Wow! she thought exhaling gustily as he fired the engine into life. It might not be such a good idea to laugh too often!

CHAPTER NINE

'THERE'S very little space to park beside the church,' Javier explained as he slowed the car to let an elderly woman dressed from head to toe in black cross the narrow street. 'We'll park the car here and walk up if that's all right with you?'

'Fine,' she replied, surprised to be consulted on the minor detail. Her agreement might not have been quite so swift if she'd realised that the village was literally cut into the side of a mountain.

Actually, as far as she was concerned there was very little space here too, so little in fact that she held her breath as he reversed the big car with what seemed like impetuous haste to her into the small space between two stone houses. Like most of those in this quaint village, they both had attractive wrought-iron balconies and so many flowers crammed in window boxes that you hardly noticed the peeling paintwork.

'Perhaps this wasn't such a good idea,' Javier observed a few minutes later as he paused once more to let her catch up with him.

'You should have left me at base camp,' she puffed.

'There is a step there; be careful…'

Kate ignored his guiding hand. 'It's all right, I can see, I'm wearing my contact lenses. I didn't bring a spare pair of glasses.'

'You have beautiful eyes.'

Kate tripped.

'It's not that far now.'

Kate decided it was preferable to shift the blame for her

stumble on her footwear than let him suspect that a casual compliment from him could make her fall flat on her face. Balancing on one leg, she extended her ankle towards him. 'If you were wearing these you wouldn't say that.'

'What possessed you to wear anything so impractical for a wedding?'

'How was I to know marriage meant a two-mile hike?' she asked indignantly. Her frivolous shoes with the pretty jewelled clip and the high spindly heels were ornamental and not suited to climbing mountains, even cobbled ones. 'If I'd known, I'd have brought my trainers.'

'You're going to injure yourself in those things,' he observed showing scant appreciation of the delicate footwear. 'Perhaps I should carry you.'

She wasn't small, but she knew his arms were more than capable of coping with the task of carrying her. Her stomach flipped over as she thought of those hard, muscular arms; it flipped some more when she thought of them holding her. She ruthlessly smothered the hot flames of excitement before they could take hold.

Taking control of herself, Kate swallowed past the constriction in her throat. 'I've got a much better idea,' she trilled brightly.

'Which is…?'

'This,' she said stepping out of the shoes. Always conscious of his superior height, suddenly slipping down to his shoulder level intensified the dramatic height differential.

He looked down at narrow feet on the dusty ground. 'You can't walk barefoot to your wedding.'

'Why not?'

'Because it's inappropriate.'

Kate laughed. 'It's a bit late for a man who'd bought a bride to start worrying about convention.'

His dark brows drew together in a disapproving line. 'I haven't bought you!' he denied harshly.

'No, just a short-term lease; I keep the freehold.'

'And no doubt you would place a very hefty price on that.'

Her eyes slewed evasively from his. 'No, actually I'd give it away free to the right man.'

Embarrassed by her own contribution to this strange exchange, Kate bent over abruptly to pick up her shoes, one in each hand, and ran a little ahead of him. 'Don't be such a stick in the mud. Go on, live a little!' she urged as she twirled around and waved the shoes at him.

A lazy smile appeared on his face as he watched her antics. Their eyes met and his smile faded, leaving a brooding, restless expression that made Kate's tummy muscles quiver. There was no knowing how long the silence that grew between them might have lasted, had not a small boy perched on a bicycle that looked way too large for him chosen that moment to race past them at a breakneck speed. Javier had to push Kate to one side to avoid a head-on collision.

He called out angrily in Spanish after the figure.

'Are you all right?'

Kate looked up into his concerned eyes and nodded, very conscious of his hands resting lightly on her shoulders.

'I'm fine, but your lovely suit is covered in dust,' she cried in dismay.

Javier glanced down at the damage. 'No matter,' he said dusting half-heartedly at the sleeve of his jacket.

Kate clicked her tongue. 'Stand still!' she instructed, examining the damage. 'It should come off,' she announced.

'Do not trouble yourself...' He stopped as Kate began to vigorously brush at the powdery layer of dust across his lapel.

Javier stood a curious smile playing about his lips. '*Lovely suit?* I thought my clothes were insipid and lacking in individuality?' One dark brow lifted. 'Have I got it right?'

Kate stopped and grimaced. 'Pretty well,' she admitted. 'If you must know, it's pretty tiresome being around someone that looks so damned perfect all the time!'

Javier looked amazed at the accusation. He looked down at himself. 'Well, I am not perfect now. Does that make me a little less *tiresome…?'*

Kate pursed her lips as she considered the matter. 'The jury's still out on that one.' Liking him could be a complication.

Javier took a second look at her pink-painted toenails and nodded. 'Go barefoot if you must, but I want one thing understood—don't expect me to take off my shoes.'

Kate grinned. 'Don't worry. Taking off your shoes is only for the advanced class. You need to start with loosening your tie…just a little.'

'You like to show me how much?' Javier asked, touching the tasteful grey silk.

Shaking her head, Kate backed off. 'No way!' If she got that close she didn't think she'd be able to resist the temptation to touch his lean jaw where already a faint shadow was just visible.

Javier accepted the rejection with a philosophical shrug; clearly he was never likely to lack candidates eager to loosen his tie. In fact, Kate found it extraordinarily easy to imagine his tie being ripped off by eager hands; in this imaginary scene his tie was closely followed by his shirt.

They walked along in silence and without Kate's heels to contend with it wasn't long before they reached the crest of the hill and the small church came into view.

'How pretty!' she exclaimed.

Javier looked pleased by her appreciation. 'Yes, isn't it? It's very old. My grandfather and grandmother were married here. They met in Madrid after the war; her parents were diplomats and she was engaged to a junior consul. There was an enormous scandal when they ran away.'

'And they ended up here?'

'Yes, she always had a soft spot for the island after that.'

There was no particular reason why this information should make her feel even worse than she already did about what they were doing, but somehow it did. Kate had been uneasy from the beginning about a church ceremony but Javier had been firm, explaining that in his grandfather's eyes a civil ceremony was not worth the paper it was printed on.

'That's why you brought me here, to impress him…?'

'My grandfather is not a man easily impressed. I just thought that this would be a nice place to be married with little fuss, but now you mention it the continuity will please the old man.'

It sounded as though Javier's grandfather was big on tradition and continuity.

'So you picked this place so that nobody you know would see us and ask awkward questions?' she concluded dully. A perfectly logical thing for him to do under the circumstances, so why did it bother her so much…?

Kate was taken by surprise when Javier caught her hands; she winced as his fingers closed tightly around her wrists, immediately he let her go.

'Did I hurt you?'

Kate didn't know what he was talking about until she saw his eyes were fixed on her wrists. 'I'll live,' she replied, rubbing her wrists.

'I do not run away and hide,' he replied clearly outraged at the suggestion. 'If anyone asks me questions I don't want to answer, I don't reply.'

'I get the picture. If bullets were whistling past your head it would be beneath your dignity to get down in the dirt with everyone else.'

'I think you'll find I have a pretty well-developed sense of self-preservation.'

'But not common sense. I see now that the idea of you keeping a low profile was a pretty daft one. You're too pig-headed.'

'If you've quite finished calling me names, come sit here.'

Kate could cope pretty well with his I'm-in-charge manner—he probably didn't even know he was doing it—but the sight of his long, tapering brown fingers curled, gently this time, around her smaller paler hands... That was another matter entirely. Kate's coping mechanisms were not built to deal with that! Such a silly thing, but she fell to pieces inside.

She didn't resist as he drew her to the side of the road, where he indicated she should sit down on a large, smooth rock. This weak capitulation was outweighed by her success in resisting the strong impulse to rub her cheek against his hand.

'Look, someone's left flowers,' she said pointing at the pretty nosegay propped up beneath a crude but beautiful statue of the Madonna.

She watched puzzled as Javier went over to the place. Careful not to disturb the flowers, he squatted down beside a small bubble of water that gurgled out of the ground into a small pool. Her covetous gaze clung with helpless fascination to the supple lines of his back; it was turning out that there was barely any part of his anatomy her fertile imagination could not spin erotic fantasies around.

'This spring is meant to have magical powers,' he explained as he cupped his hands and let them fill with the fresh water.

'What sort of magical powers?' she asked as he walked towards her, shiny drops of water falling like bright jewels from between his cupped fingers onto the parched ground below.

Javier knelt at her feet.

Finally seeing his intention, an astonished Kate drew back her feet. 'You can't...' she protested.

'I'm not marrying a woman with dirty feet.'

'I didn't think Monteros performed menial tasks.' It wasn't the menial nature of the task that bothered her, it was the uncomfortable intimacy.

'Don't provoke, Kate, just give me your damned foot.'

His tone was exasperated, nothing very lover-like about that, which ought to make her feel better...*ought!*

Reluctantly, she extended her foot.

Javier looked so long at the her slim calf and slender ankle that Kate finally cleared her throat noisily.

When he lifted his head jerkily at the sound, there was an odd, unfocused expression on his face.

The water he trickled slowly over her hot, dusty extremity was so icily cold that she gasped.

He grinned at her reaction. 'I forgot to warn you, it's cold.'

The eyes that rested on her face were not cold, they were warm. She looked hurriedly away as one of the little jolts of sexual awareness she was coming to recognise so well knifed through her body.

'Now he tells me,' she grumbled, angling her arm as casually as she could across her chest to hide the brazen thrust of her nipples. This was sexual craving of a type she'd never experienced in her life before; having come to terms with her apparent low sex drive, this transformation was hard to get her head around.

She sat there passively while he repeated the process with the other foot; it seemed to take him an eternity. If anyone had suggested this morning that having a man pour cold water over your hot feet could be a deeply erotic experience, she would have thought they were mildly deviant.

'Those magical powers you were talking about,' she asked, more from a desperate need to distract herself from the dangerous frissons of pleasure his lightest touch evoked than any genuine desire for an explanation, 'what are they?'

Javier shook his hands free of the moisture clinging to them and rose lithely to his feet, mockery danced in his eyes. 'Fertility.'

'*Oh!*'

The amused lines radiating from his eyes deepened as she blushed.

'Local folklore has it that women wanting to conceive who drink from here will bear a son,' he explained solemnly.

Kate looked at the innocent trickle of water and laughed nervously. 'Do people still believe things like that?' she joked.

Javier didn't smile back.

'Well, I'd say from the floral offering that someone does...wouldn't you...?'

'But you don't?' Kate flashed him an incredulous look at his lean, guarded features. 'Do you...?' She shook her head unable to reconcile the notion of this sophisticated man believing in a superstitious myth.

He shrugged. 'I'm not superstitious, but I respect other people's beliefs, and I do believe that we are in danger of losing many things of value by turning our backs on our roots.'

Kate was astonished; Javier was the last person in the world she would ever have imagined voicing such opinions.

'Personally, I'm quite happy to leave the fear, bigotry and superstition in the past,' she told him with a shudder.

'Are you sure it isn't your own fear that bothers

you...fear of things that you can't explain away with twenty-first century science...?' he challenged.

'Rubbish!' she denied. 'I'm just not going to campaign for a return of witch-burning.'

'Maybe you have a personal interest there.'

'Are you calling me a witch?' Kate demanded indignantly.

For a moment he stood there, looking down at the barefooted figure at his feet, hair spread like a bright nimbus around a delicately flushed face. 'I can't think of any other explanation,' he replied sardonically. 'Put your shoes on,' he added tersely, before Kate had time to puzzle over his cryptic response or even the peculiar expression on his saturnine features. 'The wedding can't start without us.'

Kate's stomach muscles quivered at the reminder. 'You're an extremely bossy man,' she remarked, staring indecisively at his outstretched hand.

A satisfied expression slid into Javier's eyes as her slim hand was placed cautiously within his, even if the manner of it getting there did remind him of a child daring to explore forbidden territory.

At the outset of this reckless enterprise all Javier had wanted was her co-operation; now gaining her trust seemed to occupy his thoughts almost as much as the attractions of her body did. He had to constantly remind himself that possessing that body would create all kinds of complications; his own body didn't always listen to these warnings.

'But I have many redeeming qualities,' he assured her as he heaved her to her feet with a grunt.

Kate dusted down her dress and sent him a wry look from under her lashes. 'I bet a female told you that.'

'More than one actually.'

'Smug, conceited, bossy *and* superstitious,' she observed with a superior expression.

'Everyone is superstitious, to some extent, be it the footballer with his lucky pair of socks or the banker who flicks salt over his shoulder,' Javier contended.

'Not me.'

'You sure about that?'

'Absolutely,' she told him with an emphatic little tilt of her chin.

'Prove it,' he challenged softly.

'*What…?*' Kate shook her head and laughed uneasily. 'There's no way I can prove it.'

'There is. Drink some water from the spring.'

'I'm not thirsty.'

A dark brow lifted. 'Like I said,' he drawled. 'Everyone is superstitious.'

Kate gritted her teeth, unable to stomach his triumphal air a second longer. 'If it's contaminated, I'll know who to blame,' she grumbled as she picked her way over the uneven ground. She extended her hand beneath the ice-cool drops and then, with a defiant glare in his direction, raised it to her mouth—the water was sweet and icy cold.

'Well…?' she challenged him, wiping the excess moisture from her lips with the back of her hand.

His darkened glance dwelt on the full, moist outline; when he spoke his voice had a husky strained quality. 'I'm impressed.'

Despite his immediate capitulation Kate was left with the uneasy feeling that somehow she'd done exactly what he wanted.

They were only a few feet away from the church, which Kate found was even prettier close to, when a stone bench built into the wall, which had previously been hidden from view by the overhanging lemon trees, came into sight.

A couple were sitting in the shade talking in quiet voices; their whole manner to one another made it clear they were not strangers. Kate felt a sudden unexpected stab of envy.

It was Kate's cry as her heel caught on a stray stone in the road that made both turn.

The woman immediately sprang to her feet, an expression of uncomplicated delight on her face; the man beside her with the dark-haired baby in his arms did so more sedately.

'*Javier!* You're here…*finally!*' The petite figure cried as she rushed forward. 'This is so exciting, I can't believe it! Marriage…!'

Beside her Kate felt Javier tense; she heard the sibilant hiss of his shocked intake of breath. Without stopping to analyse the impulse that drove her to do so, Kate caught his hand and squeezed hard.

Javier's head turned sharply he looked from Kate's concerned face, dominated by a pair of wide troubled eyes desperately trying to telegraph comfort, to their tightly clasped hands and back again. The restive glint slowly faded from his eyes and he smiled.

It was no ordinary smile. Kate caught her breath; every instinct told her this was one of those special moments. The sight of lemon trees, the scent of jasmine on a warm afternoon, would always hold a special meaning for her in future; they'd unlock this memory. She could almost hear the sound of something deep inside—maybe her reserve snapping?—as the warmth of his eyes caressed her before he turned to the other woman. There was no hint of any underlying trauma in his manner as he responded to her greeting.

'Sarah!'

Now she had time to look properly, Kate was stunned to discover the love of Javier's life, far from being the supermodel material she'd expected, was a tiny creature with big blue eyes, a cute button nose complete with freckles and an extraordinarily sweet smile. She was extremely feminine, the sort of woman that brought out the chivalrous instincts in men—they evidently had done in Javier. Kate, who had never in her life wanted to be protected by a man, experienced an irrational pang of envy.

'This is Kate,' Javier said, drawing her forwards.

You had to hand it to him, Kate conceded as she smiled stiltedly. Nobody watching him operate would guess the proprietorial pride was not the genuine article—so long as *you* remember it isn't, Katie, the spoilsport voice of common sense in her head inserted wryly.

'Kate, this is Sarah, and of course you already know Serge, and the little one is Raul. *Madre mia,* but he's grown since I saw him last,' he observed, reaching out to tentatively touch the head of the sleeping baby.

'That's because you don't come and see us nearly often enough,' the baby's mother returned reproachfully. She turned to Kate. 'Perhaps now you'll be able to make him come see us once in a while,' she appealed.

'I'll do my best.' Well, she could hardly admit her influence was nil, because it was abundantly clear that this woman thought the marriage she was about to witness was for real.

'Miss Anderson...' The swarthy-skinned man who had witnessed the worst indignities of her life nodded diffidently as their eyes met.

Kate felt an embarrassed tide of colour wash over her skin. Now here was someone who didn't, who *couldn't,* think the marriage was for real!

'Kate,' she corrected stiltedly. 'Very nice to see you again...' she lied fluently. 'And quite a surprise,' she added, throwing Javier an acid look of reproach which the rat pretended not to see, but as Sarah was nestling affectionately up to him maybe he didn't, she thought, experiencing a nasty stab of something that felt scarily like jealousy.

Her smile was bright and ever so slightly desperate as she hurriedly turned her attention back to the thick-set fig-

ure beside her. Though he didn't come right out and call
her a liar, she could tell from his expression that Serge
didn't believe in her delight at renewing their acquaintance.

Or maybe paranoia was setting in! The way today was
going it seemed best to assume the worst.

She watched as he carefully adjusted the sunhat on the
tiny head of the baby, who continued to cling limpet-like
to his massive chest. She sighed. Forget flashy cars, and as
far as she was concerned there were fewer sights more
guaranteed to thaw a woman's heart than the sight of a big,
brawny man with a tiny baby.

Javier could at least have warned her about who one of
their witnesses was to be.

The embarrassment she could cope with if she had to,
but being pitched headlong into the middle of a situation
that had all the ingredients of a Greek tragedy was another
matter!

Javier loved Serge's wife, but did Serge know…? Did
Sarah know…if so, all that touchy feely stuff with Javier
was a bit below the belt!

Talk about love triangles!

As she looked back to the previous occasions she'd seen
the two men together, acting very much as a team, Kate
couldn't recall witnessing any tension or underlying hostile
currents between them. That of course didn't necessarily
mean there was none…

'What a lovely baby.' In her experience, admiring their
offspring was always a good way to please parents, but in
this case her observations were nothing but the truth; the
sleeping child was quite beautiful.

'Well, don't I rate a hug with you these days, big
guy…?' she heard Sarah chide.

From the corner of her eye she was aware that an enthusiastic embrace was being exchanged. Worriedly she
looked at Serge and saw he was already watching them; to

her relief he seemed to view the proceedings with an air of faint indulgence.

Indulgence wasn't the first emotion she experienced when she got her first proper look at the hug-fest. She was a big fan of spontaneity and definitely no prude, but to Kate's way of thinking this was way over the top!

For someone so fragile-looking, Sarah had managed to get a pretty firm grip around Javier's neck and was pressing some vigorous kisses to his lean cheeks and mouth. If she did know of Javier's feelings for her, Sarah's actions could only be termed callous and uncaring, Kate decided indignantly. She looked away as Javier placed the fairy-like figure back on the floor, troubled by her ambivalent reaction to the spectacle.

Seeing the sparkle of tears in the other woman's eyes. Kate found it impossible to hold on to her antipathy.

'I didn't know if you'd have time so I picked these from our garden…I hope you don't mind…?' She thrust out a bunch of flowers tied together with a blue velvet ribbon and then a small package towards Kate.

'Thank you!' Kate exclaimed feeling horribly guilty about her uncharitable thoughts towards this woman who exuded a wide-eyed sweet sincerity—not qualities she'd have imagined would have attracted Javier, but then men were strange, unpredictable creatures.

'We're just so happy that Javier has found someone to make him happy.'

Kate felt increasingly uncomfortable as Serge produced a tissue for his tearful wife.

'He's the sweetest man in the world, but then why am I telling you?' she sniffed emotionally. 'You already know that…'

I know nothing!

Javier didn't respond to her flustered look of appeal in quite the way she'd anticipated.

'Kate thinks I'm bossy and arrogant, don't you, *querida?*' he drawled.

Thanks for nothing, Javier! She allowed her resentful glare to linger pointedly on his incredibly handsome, mocking face. 'Amongst other things.'

You'd have thought it was in his best interest to ensure I don't put my foot in it, but if that's the way he wants to play it, fine!

'You've known him longer than me,' Kate appealed to the other woman. 'Has he always fancied himself as an authority figure?'

Once Sarah recovered from the shock of hearing anyone speak to Javier so daringly, she let out an appreciative chuckle.

'Kate's definitely got your number, Javier,' she told him.

His brilliant eyes flashed. '*Now* you're scaring me,' he asserted sardonically.

No, I'm not, Kate thought tearing her eyes free from the hypnotic glow of his, but she was scaring herself badly!

She had no legitimate reason to wonder what it would be like to play this part for real, to conjecture on what it might feel like to actually be the loved, cherished bride Sarah thought she was. Besides, being loved by a man like Javier would be a nightmare.

A girl would have a heck of job retaining any individual identity; he would be an overwhelming and demanding lover who would not be content to fit himself in around her busy career. It would be quite a dilemma for an independent career girl to find herself in love with a man like that...luckily for her, her contractual obligation stopped short of that requirement!

She congratulated herself on her impregnable heart and felt queasy.

'Now, Kate, come and tell me everything,' Sarah suggested in a deeply alarming, cosy-girls-together sort of voice as she tried to draw Kate slightly apart from the men folk—a manoeuvre which Kate resisted stubbornly. 'Serge's been about as informative as a rock,' she continued, shooting her husband a look of affectionate exasperation. 'So how long have you two actually known one another?'

'Not long.'

Kate's evasive reply seemed to seemed to appeal to the other woman's deeply sentimental nature; her round kittenish eyes softened.

'Time's not a factor when you meet the right person, is it?' she sighed soulfully. 'Where are you going to live? Don't worry about the language thing, Kate... I couldn't speak Spanish when I came here, but I'm fluent now... aren't I, Serge?'

'You are indeed, *querida*,' he agreed smoothly. 'I hate to interrupt, but the padre will be waiting...'

'All right, I can take a hint.'

'Only when it's broad,' Kate was amazed to hear her sober-looking mate drily quip.

'Very funny... So I talk a lot,' Sarah admitted. 'But at least let her open the parcel. No, it's for you, not him,' Sarah insisted with a secretive smile when Kate went to hand the parcel to Javier 'Open it now,' she coaxed.

Kate shrugged and handed Javier her sweet-smelling bouquet instead. If she hadn't been so distracted she'd have laughed at the sight of him standing there staring at the flowers as if they were about to bite him.

'I can't accept this!' She gasped when a cobwebby lace mantilla was finally revealed; it was exquisite and clearly very old. Shaking her head she pushed it towards the other girl who held up her hands.

'It's not really mine.' She glanced towards Javier. 'I was just borrowing it. Javier let me use it on my wedding day. It was his mother's; you should wear it, Kate.'

'I...' How to explain to a hopeless romantic who was clearly under the impression she was witnessing a love match, that she was the last person in the world Javier would want to see wearing a family heirloom?

Javier solved her dilemma by taking the lace veil from her hands. He tilted her chin up towards him and arranged the delicate folds carefully over her bright hair.

'She looks so beautiful!' said Sarah. Her enthusiastic clapping stilled abruptly as she remembered the sleeping baby. An anxious look revealed he was still soundly sleeping.

'Very beautiful,' Javier agreed softly, putting the flowers back into her trembling hands.

Kate's lashes lifted as, lips parted slightly, she looked directly into his eyes—major mistake! Even knowing his performance was for Sarah's sake, she couldn't halt the rippling progress of the spasm that contracted all the fine muscles across her abdomen. She snatched her eyes away, her breathing all askew.

Oh, help! she thought, trying to smother the prickles of sexual excitement that coursed through her sensitised body as she saw the church door swing open. *I can't do this!*

Against all expectation a sense of deep calm descended on Kate as she entered the tiny church. Perhaps she was affected by the atmosphere of cool and quiet? Perhaps she had accepted her fate? But whatever the reason, when the time came she made her responses in a clear composed voice interrupted only by the fretful whimpers of Raul. Kate was hardly aware of the off stage distractions so totally focused was she on the ceremony and the man beside her. If anything it was Javier who looked unexpectedly tense, perhaps he was worried that she'd wimp out at the last minute?

She'd expected to feel as if she was taking part in travesty, a cruel parody of what should be one of the most important events in a woman's life, but when Javier lifted her veil it felt natural and *right* to kiss him back.

Back out in the sunshine, on the arm of her husband—*husband!*—the reality of her situation kicked in and her head literally spun.

She found it almost impossible to concentrate when an embarrassed Sarah apologised profusely for Raul. 'He needs to be fed, don't you darling?' she cooed, taking the baby from her husband. 'Does anyone mind if I find a quiet corner…?'

Her husband looked at her anxiously. 'You can manage, *mi esposa?*' he asked.

'You can do many things quite beautifully, darling, but produce milk isn't one of them.'

At any other time the sight of big beefy Serge blushing would have afforded Kate considerable amusement, but at that moment all her efforts were concentrated on putting one foot in front of the other. The physical and emotional demands of the last two days were finally catching up with her.

'I think I need to sit down!' she gasped faintly.

Javier took one look at her ghostly pallor and immediately scooped her up into his arms as if she were a child. *'Por Dios!'* he exclaimed as Kate's head fell limply against his shoulder.

Javier cursed quietly under his breath. A man famed for his legendary cool, he wasn't accustomed to finding his wits flying out the window in moments of crisis, but for several seconds his mind was a total blank. What if this was some sort of delayed reaction to the head injury…? Much more likely it was a reaction to being forced into a marriage that was repugnant to her, he thought grimly.

'This is so stupid.'

Javier watched as her blue-veined eyelids fluttered, as if it took all her effort to lift them.

'Perhaps I should have eaten breakfast,' she murmured vaguely.

'There's no *perhaps* about it!' he thundered, relieved that the blue tinge around her lips had lessened. 'I hope you are not one those foolish women who starve themselves,' he added suspiciously.

Lifting her head from its resting place on his shoulder took all her effort. 'Do I look like one?' she asked, gloomily contrasting her own generous proportions with Sarah's delicate ethereal build.

'You look...' he began in a goaded voice, only to break off abruptly, his expression that of a man who'd just suffered a body blow. 'Like a ghost,' he finished hoarsely.

'Take her to the house, Javier. A lie-down in the cool will help. Sarah has prepared a small supper; we thought you might like...'

'I'm not sure, but thank you, Serge. If only I'd tried to get the car all the way up here.'

'Leave her with me, Javier, while you get the car,' Serge urged after thoughtfully scrutinising his friend's tense, strained expression.

Javier was extremely reluctant, but he was finally persuaded to relinquish his burden who by now was proclaiming herself quite capable of walking to the car under her own steam.

'You will stay with her, Serge?'

'I won't let her out of my sight for a second,' his friend soothed.

'This is silly!' Kate protested as she was placed beside Serge on the stone bench. 'I was light-headed for a minute, that's all.'

'You will do as I ask!' Javier announced imperiously.

'*Dream on,*' Kate muttered under her breath.

His brows arched. 'You said something, *querida?*'

'Nothing you'd like.'

'I never doubted it,' he gritted back with a glittering smile before he strode off. Kate watched until he disappeared from view; when he did a long tremulous sigh escaped her lips.

'You care for him…?'

Kate jumped at the amazed accusation voiced by the man beside her. 'Pardon?'

Serge calmly repeated his observation.

Kate, furiously ducking and diving from the truth, found it hard to meet his level dark gaze. 'I don't know him; how can I care for him?' She laughed at the absurdity of the notion. 'Javier married me so that he can take control of the company. And if you didn't know that, I'm in big trouble. He'll probably accuse me of industrial espionage, this time!' she predicted wryly.

'Is that what he told you…? That he was worried about his inheritance.' Serge shook his head and looked amused. 'I take it you've never met Felipe.'

'We don't exactly move in the same circles.' Kate was puzzled by Serge's peculiar reaction to her shocking explanation.

'If you'd ever seen Felipe with Javier you would know that he'd *never* disinherit him; it just isn't an option,' he stated positively.

'They've argued,' Kate explained. 'He wants Javier to marry some girl…'

Serge dismissed this with a shrug. 'Sure, they clash occasionally, it's inevitable. They are both strong-willed, but Felipe adores Javier. Did you know he brought him up after his mother's death?'

Something in his tone caught Kate's attention; she was good at picking up the things people *didn't* say. 'How did she die?'

'She took an overdose, Javier was only ten at the time, he found her.'

'How awful!' Kate gasped, sickened by the horrifying thought of a ten-year-old child carrying that image around in his head for the rest of his life. Her tender heart ached; poor Javier. 'Is his father dead, too?'

Serge shook his head. 'No. He was overcome with guilt after his wife's death; she adored him you see, but…he was a womaniser and not a very discreet one. He drifted for some years. I believe he lives on a ranch the family owns in Venezuela these days, but he keeps a very low profile. He left Javier with Felipe; to all intents and purposes Felipe is the only father he remembers.'

'But I don't u-understand…' Kate stammered, absorbing the implications of Javier's tragic family history. 'Why would he marry me if what you say is true? If he knows his grandfather won't disinherit him?'

'I'm sure he had his reasons.'

This clearly was enough for him, but not for Kate, whose head was spinning.

'He lied to me!' she wailed.

'Maybe, but I think he…cares for you.'

Good God, the man had clearly been infected by his wife's terminal sentimentality. 'Cares for me? Are you mad? You know how we met—all of forty-eight hours ago. He doesn't even like me!' she cried.

Serge responded with an infuriatingly enigmatic smile. 'I loved Sarah the moment I saw her.'

'So did Javier, and much good it did him!' Kate retorted recklessly. 'Oh, God!' she gasped, clapping her hand over her mouth. 'I didn't mean…I'm s-so sorry…' she stammered.

'It's all right, you are not telling me anything I didn't already know.'

Good God, had they discussed it? Now that was a mind-boggling proposition.

'And you don't mind...?'

This man had to be a very unusual Spanish male if he didn't mind another man lusting after his wife, and to Kate he appeared to have the full complement of possessive traits.

'It doesn't worry you?' No matter how much you trusted a friend, wouldn't there always be a nagging doubt?

'What should I worry about, Kate?'

Kate shook her head; she could hardly ask him if he wasn't worried that, despite his lofty ideals, one day Javier might succumb to temptation and make a move; having experienced Javier's skills on the kissing front, Kate could imagine that even a happily married woman might be hard put to resist.

'Sarah has always been unaware of the strength of Javier's feelings and I'd like to stay that way. I know he will never mention it to her...' He looked at Kate expectantly.

'I won't say a word,' she promised.

'Good. Let me tell you a story, and perhaps you'll understand why Javier will always be welcome in my house. When Sarah was young she contracted a disease, a pelvic inflammatory condition she contracted from a lover.'

'Chlamydia.'

'You have heard of it; I hadn't when she told me,' he admitted. 'It left her unable to conceive naturally, you see, and she was afraid that I would reject her,' he recalled with an incredulous smile that wrung Kate's heart. To her way of thinking, Sarah was an extremely fortunate individual to inspire that sort of love—in not just one man but two!

'I am not a wealthy man,' Serge continued.

Which begged the question of how he became a close friend of Javier.

'And IVF treatment is not cheap. We scraped together enough money,' he explained. 'But our expectations were frankly unrealistic and when we were not successful it hit Sarah hard; she became very depressed.' Kate could see that thinking of these dark days clearly affected him deeply.

'But you have Raul now.'

His dark eyes flashed. 'Yes, we have Raul—*thanks to Javier.*'

Kate swallowed her impatience and a desire to shake the information out of him as he lapsed once more into a reflective silence.

Finally she was unable to contain her curiosity.

'Javier helped somehow…?' she prompted.

He nodded. 'Javier arranged for us to spend some time with her family in England, and after Sarah was feeling better he arranged for us to see one of the leading infertility experts in England. The doctor was frank about our chances. Because of Sarah's previous eating disorder as well, the odds were not on our side. After much soul-searching we decided to go ahead with the treatment; it helped enormously that Sarah had the support of her family this time, and Raul was the result.'

Kate was stunned by this extraordinary tale of altruism, made all the more so by the fact that if Javier had wanted Sarah all he'd needed to do was stand by and do nothing while her marriage had disintegrated under the strain.

God, what a frustratingly complex person he was. Clearly there was a hell of a lot more to Javier Montero than your average macho male. Knowing all this didn't alter the fact that her main qualification as a prospective wife had been the fact she didn't love him! It was something she had better remember the next time she felt inclined to argue with him.

It was just as well there was very little traffic because Javier had effectively blocked the road with his car, Kate was in the middle of pointing out the inconsiderate nature of such behaviour when Sarah appeared breathlessly at their side.

'Oh, Kate, are you all right?' she cried.

'I'm totally fine,' Kate responded. 'Don't let the fact I'm being hauled about like a sack of potatoes fool you; Javier wouldn't let me walk,' she explained, treating him to an exasperated scowl.

'Are you sure? Serge said you fainted.' A flash of inspiration flickered across her face. 'Gosh, you're not pregnant, are you?'

'P-pregnant…? *No,* I'm definitely not!' she returned, not daring to look at Javier.

The petite blonde's face fell. 'That's a pity. It would be nice if there wasn't too big a gap between Raul and your first baby.'

Kate could hardly believe it when Javier added in a provocative husky undertone that made her tummy muscles quiver, 'Not yet, anyway, but she did take a drink from the spring on the way here, didn't you, *querida*?'

Kate shot him a look that she hoped made clear he'd better quit all that sexy *querida* nonsense, or else. 'It was hot and dusty,' she defended.

Sarah looked sympathetic. 'Don't tease, Javier, can't you see you're embarrassing the girl?' she remonstrated. 'I hope I haven't offended you, Kate,' she worried. 'It was just you had the quiet ceremony, and I thought maybe…?'

'We *had* to get married?' Kate responded bluntly. 'Well, we didn't, but…' No matter how hard she racked her brains she couldn't think of a single halfway plausible explanation for the hole in a corner nature of the ceremony.

Unexpectedly Javier came to her rescue.

'My grandfather is not well, Sarah. It wouldn't have been fair to put him through the strain of an elaborate wedding, but we couldn't wait,' he explained, giving a very authentic impression of an eager lover. 'Could we, *querida*?' he purred.

On the receiving end of a caressing look that reduced her to a quivering wreck, Kate nodded numbly.

'Oh I'm so sorry about your grandfather, Javier. I didn't know.'

Javier brushed aside her embarrassed apologies. 'I'm sorry Kate's not well enough to come to supper...a rain check?'

'Definitely,' Sarah beamed.

CHAPTER TEN

UNLIKE the suite at the resort, this one had two very large bedrooms. Kate didn't have any possessions to put in the one allocated to her, but she soon discovered that Javier had anticipated this. A comprehensive array of clothes in her size, all with expensive designer labels she coveted, were hanging up in the walk-in wardrobe and more were neatly folded on the shelves. As she fingered the fine silk of a matching set of bra and minuscule pants, she tried not to think about how he knew her bra size!

Still a bit sleepy-eyed and grouchy after her nap in the car, she entered the sitting room carrying a bar of soap which was the same herbal-scented brand she preferred to use—no coincidence, she was sure.

'How did you know…?'

'Meticulous research,' Javier explained languidly as he took a sip from the glass of whisky he was nursing. The ice chinked as he saluted her with it. 'A shower might refresh you…' His eyes slid over her cream dress and ended up on her bare toes before making the return journey to her face. 'Or would you like some food brought up?'

In other words, I look like a dish rag!

'A bar of soap I can live with,' she gritted unsmilingly. 'But I can't accept clothes from you.'

'Millions of pounds you can accept but a few clothes you can't? I'm sure there's some logic in there somewhere, but I must admit it escapes me momentarily.'

'That's not the same thing and you know it!'

'You do need to dress for the part; as my wife you will be expected to project a certain image.'

'I'm sorry if you don't like my clothes sense but I'm not about to be made over into some plastic bimbo clone!' she announced, planting her hands firmly on her hips as she glared belligerently across at him. 'So you can cancel the hair appointments and the image consultant,' she told him quiveringly. 'That wasn't part of the deal. You can't say you weren't warned—I told you I was poor value for money—but you went ahead and married me anyway. So if you're ashamed of me in front of your posh friends and family, *too bad!*'

Her piece said, Kate experienced a sudden and strong desire to burst into tears…as if it mattered what he thought of her?

Javier examined the antagonistic glitter in her eyes and let out a long, slow whistle. Sitting forward in his chair he placed his glass on the gleaming surface of an antique metal banded oak chest beside him.

'I knew you couldn't bring luggage with you without causing comment, so it seemed sensible to arrange for some clothes in your sizes brought here,' he told her quietly. 'I merely asked for them to be classic, simple and understated, like the things I have seen you wear,' he revealed with what seemed genuine admiration.

'*Oh!*' Looking down at her crumpled linen shift Kate could only wonder at his taste.

'If I'd wanted to play Svengali,' he added drily, 'I would not have chosen you as a subject; you are probably the *least* malleable person I have ever known. It is true however that we will attend functions where people will be expensively dressed. You may wear chain-store clothes if that is what you wish.' His broad shoulders lifted in a negligent shrug. 'But I did think you might find it less of an ordeal if you blended in. I see no reason for you to suffer financially to that end.' Having shot down in flames just about every aspect of her complaint and made her feel petty and un-grateful in the bargain, he picked up his drink.

As he raised the glass to his lips, he continued to study her unblinkingly over the rim. 'Incidentally, I like your hair.'

His eyes held a possessive gleam as he examined the silvery tumble of soft waves that had unexpectedly excited his admiration.

'I shall take the risk of you rushing out to cut it off, or dye it purple to establish your total disdain for my opinion, and admit I would not like it at all if you changed anything about it,' he told her softly.

Kate gulped and regrouped. 'Maybe I was a bit hasty about the clothes, but you should have told me we'd be coming here.' She pushed her fringe from her eyes; it felt lank and floppy, which made his reaction to it all the more amazing in her eyes. The picture of a glowing bride she was not!

Despite the fact he had discarded his jacket and his tie was loosened, Javier still looked as fresh and vital as ever.

'My parents will be worried…' God, she still had to tell them. That should be fun; what'll I say…? *Mum and Dad, I got married yesterday, but don't worry, it's not going to change my life…* Only it already had, she realised as her eyes were drawn to the sleek figure slouched in the chair.

Javier had to be the only man in the universe who could slouch elegantly!

'I left a message for them explaining that you were feel-ing much better and I was taking you to visit friends and we'd probably be staying overnight.'

'A lie for every occasion.'

'No lie; Serge is a friend and he is manager here.'

'Oh, is that how you know him?'

'My grandparents had a villa about a mile from here; we

would spend summers here.' His soft reflective smile suggested these were happy memories.

Kate found she was fiercely glad about that. After what Serge had told her about the tragedies in his childhood she was glad that Javier had some good memories. She swallowed as an image of a small, lonely boy materialised in her head—a boy with golden skin and blue eyes; the image made her heart ache.

'Serge's mother was their housekeeper,' he explained. 'We used to run wild together. This very spot was one of our favourite places; it was just a ruin at the time, and probably dangerous into the bargain, but you don't want to hear about my childhood.'

Actually, she did. Kate was horrified to discover that she was in fact interested in everything about him! She ate up the details like an addict.

'You are happy about the arrangements I made…?'

'You seem to have anticipated everything…'

'Not everything. I thought I had…' he mused contemplating the bottom of his glass through narrowed eyes. His long lashes suddenly lifted. 'But I was wrong.'

Being the sudden focus of his curiously intense blue gaze unsettled Kate, who was already incredibly jumpy. Unable to bear his scrutiny any longer, she turned her back on him and pretended a great interest in the fine examples of local art hanging on the wall, when all the time all she was actually conscious of was Javier.

All her senses were finely tuned to his smallest gesture, the slightest inflection in his voice; in fact, she was so hyper-focused there was a strong possibility that she was seeing and hearing things that weren't there.

'You're not happy that I left the message?'

'It's not that, it's just… Well, I'm used to doing things for myself. It feels strange to have someone else speak on my behalf.'

'Ah, yes, the independent career woman.'

Kate spun around angrily. 'Don't you dare patronise me...or...'

'If you're going to threaten, Kate,' he advised her smoothly, 'it's always more effective if you decide beforehand with what or how you're going to intimidate your victim. With married people I believe the withdrawal of your sexual favours is a popular method. Of course,' he mused silkily, 'you have to grant them first...'

Was the hint of a question in his voice or a figment of her fertile and overheated imagination? The remotest possibility that he was actually suggesting they consummate their union had her heart beating like a drum.

She sharply veered her thoughts from the dangerous direction they were taking. 'I'm just saying...' Damned if I know what I was saying! She exhaled and started again. 'It would just have been nice to be consulted. I might have felt less...'

'Less what?'

Her hand went to the base of her throat as their eyes met, she could feel the heavy throb of a pulse there. 'Manipulated,' she ground out.

'Is that how I make you feel?'

Out of control, sexually depraved...*needy*...? The list went on and on!

She shrugged and tucked a stray strand of hair behind her ear. 'Forget it; I was just shocked to wake up and find myself here.'

She hadn't been shocked at first, he recalled; that had come a few moments later when the wary light in her eyes had resurfaced.

In those very first moments after he'd gently shaken her awake there had been no concealing caution, her velvety eyes had been filled with sleepy, sensual invitation that had taken his breath clear away. In that brief, unguarded moment she'd looked up at him, all softness and warmth, glowing as if lit from within.

The recollection of it made his body respond as it had done at the time, when all he'd wanted to do was pull her beneath him and kiss her senseless in a prelude to removing every stitch of clothing from her delicious soft body, then he'd taste every inch of that too. He wouldn't allow himself to satisfy his hunger completely, though, not until she was begging him to…drawing out the pleasure until it hurt.

When she had reached out and touched his cheek, her fingertips light and delicate as they ran over the stubble on his jaw, Javier had been forced to reassess the timescale of his plans. Javier understood the power of sex, but the hunger that gripped him at that moment was more urgent than any he could recall.

A small pucker had appeared between her feathery brows as her hand fell away. 'You're not a dream,' she breathed in the moment before she realised where she was, and who he was.

Javier, not a man given to wishing, was left wishing hard that he was the man she had taken him for. A man whose existence he discovered he deeply resented.

Kate stepped backwards as Javier suddenly levered himself up from the chair in one lithe, fluid motion. She watched as he began to move around the room, his whole manner radiating restless energy… Perhaps he was feeling the confines of this paper marriage already?

Perhaps regret was responsible for the brooding expression on his face she speculated as she watched him push open the double doors that led out onto a flower-decked wrought-iron balcony. As he turned back to face her, Kate's breath caught; standing there with the light breeze ruffling the smooth glossy outline of his dark hair, drawing the fabric of his shirt tightly over his torso, he made a simply magnificent figure.

The frown line deepened above his classical nose as his eyes skimmed her motionless figure. 'I thought you would welcome an opportunity to…adjust to our…arrangements before you face your family.' A wry expression drifted across his face. 'I know I do. Surely you didn't think we'd be going back there tonight? That you would be sharing a room with your sister?'

'Well, actually, I was so busy wondering how I was going to get through the wedding itself,' she revealed ingenuously, 'that I hadn't thought as far as the honeymoon.'

In fact, Kate, you haven't thought much at all! With a sigh she slumped despondently into a tapestry-covered easy chair.

'Have I said something funny…?' she asked as he smiled one of those lop-sided numbers that she found not only wildly attractive but impossible to interpret. 'I'm not speaking honeymoon in the literal sense, of course,' she hastily clarified.

'You know it will do my over-inflated ego a power of good to be in your company…' If he hadn't had to fend off some determined candidates, Javier might have been forced to reconsider the widely held belief amongst his envious contemporaries that there were any number of women who might not consider marriage to him was something to be *endured!*

'Have you any idea how long we might have to…'

'Cohabit?'

'I was going to say pretend to be married,' she corrected tartly—cohabit had an uncomfortably intimate sound to it.

'We *are* married and I have the papers to prove it.'

'Not properly!' she countered crossly.

'I had noticed.'

Kate took the gutless route and acted as if she was oblivious to the challenge in his eyes. 'This is a very nice hotel,' she observed, sweeping past him onto the balcony which looked out onto a sunny courtyard and the mountains beyond. Hands on the wrought-iron scroll work, she leaned over to get a better look at the fountain beneath. The only sound was the trickle of the water and the distant hum of bees going about their business; it was a lazy, relaxing sound.

'When we were trawling through the holiday brochures, I wanted to stay here, but I was overruled.' Eyes closed, she lifted her face to the sun.

It didn't take a genius to figure out by whom; as far as Javier could see the little sister with her charming manner and shallow smile seemed to get exactly what she wanted. Worse still, Kate seemed to be quite resigned to taking second place. As far as he was concerned, if there was ever a woman who ought to take first place it was Katherine M. Anderson.

Kate didn't realise that he'd followed her until she felt his breath against her neck.

'*Coward...*' he whispered softly.

Kate started so violently that for a moment she lost her balance and tipped too far forwards until only her toes were still on terra firma.

'*Por Dios!*' Javier cried harshly as he hauled her bodily back from the balustrade. He turned her roughly around to face him.

The hand he planted in the small of her back brought her hard up against his body; the one twisted into her hair tilted her face up to his. Every point of contact between them was an exquisite kind of torture as her receptive nerve-endings came to life. As far as Kate was concerned, colliding head-on with his blazing blue eyes was a far more terrifying experience than nearly falling fifty feet onto cobbles.

Held this close, she was aware not only of his amazing strength, but the waves of fury vibrating through his lean, hard body too. In his heightened emotional state he unconsciously slipped back into his mother tongue. Kate stood there in a blank condition of shock while a hot tide of furious Spanish washed over her.

His perfect mouth twisted. 'Are you trying to kill yourself?' he demanded thickly, apparently unaware that she hadn't understood a word of his tirade to that point.

'Why, are you offering to do it for me?'

She saw straight off—it was hard not to!—that her defensive flippancy had not gone down well. Javier drew a sharp breath that made his muscled torso strain hard against the fabric of his shirt.

'Do not tempt me!' The irony of this advice brought a self derisive twist to his lips… *Temptation.* His eyes moved hungrily over her face. He had always prided himself on his self-control but her mere presence was temptation.

The crackling sexual tension between them was suddenly like a physical presence in the room. Without warning, Kate's legs turned to rubber; if he released her now she'd certainly slide gracelessly to the floor, but he showed no sign of releasing her. If anything, his grip tightened. She felt as though an invisible hand was inside her chest, squeezing her heart; the pressure made it hard to breathe.

'It was your fault,' she contended belligerently. 'You shouldn't have crept up on me like that.'

Javier's nostrils flared as he inhaled sharply. 'You are the most infuriating woman!' he exploded, lowering his dark face down towards hers.

His burning glance dropped to her mouth and stayed there. The fingers in her hair tightened as his rapid respirations grew slower and slower…until he didn't seem to be breathing at all.

She ran her tongue nervously over her dry lips and a shocking groan of pain was wrenched from Javier's throat.

'S…sorry.' Without being precisely aware of how, Kate

knew that she was in some way responsible for his apparent agony.

It was her turn to moan when he suddenly touched his thumb to her mouth and slowly traced the still moist outline of her tender lips. Kate shivered as hot desire drenched her like a cloud burst.

'*Please...*' she whispered brokenly just before his mouth came crashing down on hers.

Kate opened her mouth, wanting the taste of him in her mouth, wanting to feel his hard, vital body against hers, in fact just *wanting* him! There was an element of desperation and driving urgency in his whisky-flavoured kiss that excited her beyond bearing.

She twisted her fingers deep into the dark hair on his nape, drawing herself upwards so that her hips were sealed to his, so that her heavy aching breasts were flattened against his chest, so that his hard arousal ground into her belly.

Eyes squeezed shut, she moved restlessly as his lips moved in her hair, over her eyelids, her neck, across her collar bone, before he returned his attention to her mouth. He kissed her as though he would drain her.

When he finally drew back, 'You are so beautiful,' she gasped reverently as she began to press her lips to the brown column of his neck. Her fingers plucked feverishly at the buttons of his shirt. It was a clumsy hit-and-miss process, her hands were shaking so hard, but even so in a matter of seconds there was a gap big enough for her to slide her fingers through. She gave a sigh of relief as her flattened palms slid across his skin; it was satiny and firm, just the way she had imagined it, only better!

She bent her head and pressed her lips to the exposed area of firm, golden flesh.

There were feverish streaks of dull colour across his cheekbones and his smile was fierce and predatory as he urgently took her face between his two hands and looked with a rapt expression deep into her passion glazed eyes.

'I want you,' he gritted.

'Then what are you waiting for?' she sobbed. 'A written invitation? *Touch me!*'

'Where?'

'Anywhere…everywhere…!'

A smile of male triumph spread over his taut features. 'Like this…?' His hands left a trail of white heat as they moved over her skin.

'Exactly like that,' she sighed voluptuously. Eyes closed, lips parted, Kate's head fell back; the intensity of the feelings coursing through her was like wild white fire in her veins.

His eyes didn't leave her aroused face as he slid the long zip of her dress all the way down. Kate's eyelids lifted as she felt the fabric slip over her shoulders. Gathering momentum, the fabric pooled around her feet. Beneath it she wore a lacy bra and pants.

'My arm…' she began, revealing a vulnerability she didn't even admit to herself. Of course he'd say the scars were irrelevant, they were part of her, but deep down did his stomach tighten with disgust…?

'Don't worry,' he soothed with a smouldering smile. 'I will get around to your little scars, too. I intend to kiss every inch of you…' he elaborated, in reply to her confused expression. Kate shivered as erotic images flashed across her consciousness. His dark head poised above her quivering body, her pink engorged nipples disappearing into his mouth…

He drew a light line between her straining breasts with the tip of his finger.

'I like a man with ambitious goals.'

Her shivers became full-blown febrile shudders when he dropped down onto his knees before her.

Kate stood there gazing in disbelief at the top of his dark head as he licked his way across the soft curve of her stomach; muscles she didn't know she had started quivering. The softness inside her grew more aggressive, more demanding, as his caresses drove her to the edge of reason for the first time in her life.

When he wrenched down the stretchy lace that sheathed her breasts so that the soft, warm, coral-tipped mounds of flesh spilled out, Kate gave an aching needy cry as his big hands curved greedily over the quivering peaks, drawing them into his mouth.

At first, neither of them noticed the ringing of the phone above their own needy murmurs. When they did, by unspoken mutual agreement they ignored it, but finally the constant shrill chime just couldn't be ignored.

Javier swore in his native tongue and ran a frustrated hand over his sweat slick forehead. His shirt hung open to the waist, exposing his finely muscled torso.

'I will be back,' he promised, levering himself upright.

Believing that was the only thing that made the brief separation bearable for Kate, who sank weakly down to her knees.

'If you don't, I'll come after you,' she promised, watching him cross the room, taking incredible pleasure from something as simple as the way he moved, the sheer animal grace of his stride, the delicious quiver of finely toned muscle beneath firm flesh... The combination sent a stab of intense sexual longing through her aching body.

Seeing the grim expression on his dark, hard-edged features as he lifted the phone to his ear, Kate felt a fleeting sympathy for the person the other end of the line—only fleeting, she was too conscious of the empty ache inside her to empathise for long with the person responsible for this untimely interruption.

Even though the conversation was conducted totally in

Spanish Javier hadn't been speaking for long before she knew that something was wrong—*seriously* wrong.

By the time he put the phone down Kate was seated on the edge of the sofa, her hands folded primly in her lap. As he approached she was glad she'd haphazardly pulled on her clothes. She knew her instincts had been right; the window of opportunity had passed her by. Javier wasn't about to become her lover.

'My grandfather has died.' He sounded chillingly matter-of-fact.

Kate gasped. 'But I thought he had...'

'It wasn't the cancer,' he interposed swiftly. 'His plane crashed. Somewhat ironic?'

'I'm so sorry, Javier.' If anything, her sympathy seemed to make him retreat farther from her. Looking at his remote profile, it was hard to believe that this was the same warm, passionate man who only moments before had introduced her to a sensual world she hadn't even known existed. It looked as if he wouldn't be taking her there any time soon...if ever!

Maybe ignorance wasn't such a bad thing. At least then she wouldn't have any idea what she was missing.

'I'm needed.'

'Of course you are.' But who do *you* need her heart cried, as she she stood there self-contained and in control. Who comforts you?

'The private jet, the *other* private jet,' he corrected himself with a display of dark irony. 'Is coming to pick me up. I'll be leaving first thing in the morning.'

Kate's normally sharp brain was slow to make the connections...I am leaving, not we are leaving, but of course everything had changed he no longer had any reason to pretend.

And that leaves me where...? Redundant, no longer

needed. He doesn't need a wife now; he doesn't need me. An image of his strong face driven by desire materialised in her head; his need had not been in question at that moment!

'You must be pretty gutted that you married me. If only you'd waited a day longer...'

His mouth twisted. 'One of life's little ironies,' he agreed unsmilingly.

'Why did you marry me, Javier? Serge said there was no way your grandfather would have disinherited you...'

'That's true,' he conceded. 'I pretended to take his threats seriously; it required very little effort on my part. Playing the heartless despot was one his pleasures in life.'

His expression as he spoke of his grandfather brought tears to her eyes. 'Then why...?'

'I wanted to make his last days happy ones,' he explained simply.

'So what happens now...to me...?'

A deep silence grew around her hasty question—one that Javier showed no inclination to break. The longer it lasted, the more deeply embarrassed Kate felt. *He's just learnt his grandfather has died and all I'm bothered about is where it leaves me—how selfish does that sound, Kate...?*

'I know you've got a lot of other things to think about, but I was just wondering...'

His hard voice sliced through her stumbling explanation. 'What do you want to happen, Kate?'

The abrupt question shook her. '*Me...?* Her slender shoulders shrugged and a small frown appeared between her eyebrows. 'I suppose I want things to go back to the way they were...?' *Suppose...?* Where had the suppose come from? She smiled staunchly and tried to put a bit of conviction into her tone. 'I mean, it's not even as if anybody need ever know what happened.' *Only I will.*

Suddenly Kate knew without question that things could

never go back to the way they were because she had been altered by events of the last couple of days, and most of all by her contact with this man.

A possibility she'd been doing her best to avoid needed facing. She might have fallen a little bit in love with him…was it possible to be a little bit in love? No, came the bleak reply, at least not if Javier was the man in question! *Oh, God…!*

'As you wish.' He shrugged in an offhand manner that drove home painfully to Kate that his lovemaking had been nothing more than an opportunist response to the signals she'd been broadcasting. 'I will arrange transport for you back to your hotel.'

'Thank you.'

His eyes lifted to her face and the pain she saw in his eyes was so profound that she raised her hand towards him in an unthinking gesture of comfort.

It was a gesture that he seemed to view with disdain, if not distaste. Under the cold regard of his eyes her hand fell away.

'If you'll excuse me, I have to ring my sister. She doesn't know yet and I'd like to be the one to tell her. It will be hard for her.'

Kate had lain for hours in her room, her body rigid and tense as she listened to the sound of Javier pacing up and down in his own room. Her empathy with his pain was like a knife in her chest, and her inability to do anything about it twisted the blade.

She genuinely thought no feeling in the world could be worse until the pacing stopped and there was ominous silence. That was when her imagination kicked in. Javier was a strong man, but strong men were notoriously bad when it came to expressing emotion. When those emotions finally escaped people could behave in ways quite out of character.

After half an hour of imagining his silent suffering she could bear it no longer.

If he was asleep, fine, she could just slip away and he would never know she'd been there; if not...well, she'd work out the what's if and when she came to them. She'd know he was all right and that was what she needed.

He wasn't asleep.

When Kate pushed open the door Javier was sitting on the bed, still fully clothed, his head in his hands. Suddenly being here didn't seem a good idea; she backed up and was actually reaching for the door handle when he revealed he was aware of her presence.

'You should be asleep.'

'I...I could hear you moving around.' He looked so haggard it hurt. She wanted to rush to him and throw her arms around him, but the hostility he was radiating stopped her.

'I'm sorry I disturbed you. I will be quiet...'

'I don't care about that!' she ground out in frustration. He was broadcasting so much pain she wanted to cry, Let me take it away for a little while. This approach would almost certainly have been rejected so Kate had to rethink her strategy.

'Then what do you care about? Ah, I see, my *agony*— you feel pity.' His lip curled derisively. 'You wish to comfort me. By offering me the comfort of your lovely body, perhaps...?' A muscle in his lean cheek jerked as his bold glance roved with insulting familiarity over her lightly clad body.

Kate's chin went up. 'You won't get rid of me that easily,' she declared coolly.

Inside she wasn't nearly so confident; inside she was a mass of painful insecurity. Throwing yourself at the man you loved when you knew that your feelings were not reciprocated was not a light-hearted step to take!

She saw Javier's eyes widen. He flattened his palms

against his thighs and, leaning forwards heavily, shook his head. 'What do you think you're doing?'

'What does it look like?' she replied as she eased the shoe-string straps of her nightgown over her shoulders. Taking a deep breath, she released her grip and let the fabric fall into a silken pool around her feet.

Javier released a long shuddering hiss.

A defiant glint in her eyes she stepped away from the fabric.

His burning gaze held all the distinguishing hallmarks of compulsion as it roamed over her slim pale flesh. '*Dios mio,*' he breathed in a shaken tone. 'I do not require a sacrifice.'

'Actually, Javier, I'm not thinking about what *you* want, but what I want…what I *need*,' she added in a driven, quivering voice. 'You started something earlier…' God, what are you doing, Kate? a horrified voice in her head asked— *this isn't you!*

But it is me, she realised, smiling. I have never been more *me!* Relief and a fresh flood of confidence surged through her.

'I have not forgotten,' Javier choked, seeing her lovely face through a shimmering haze of heat. His eyes dropped. '*Madre mia,* but you are perfect!' he exclaimed with husky, gloating appreciation.

'Perfect, no, but I am here and I'm getting cold,' she revealed from between chattering teeth—a condition that had nothing to do with the temperature and a lot to do with the trauma of throwing herself at the most gorgeous man in the world with no upfront guarantee he wouldn't laugh in her face.

'I think I can do something about that.' Off the bed in one lithe bound, he picked her up as though she were a size eight and not a size twelve going on fourteen, and carried her over to the bed.

She closed her eyes, feeling his mouth touch the pulse spot at the base of her throat. She let out a deep sigh as his big, clever hands moved over her heavy, aching breasts then across her stomach. One stayed there, resting softly on the feminine curve of her belly, while the other boldly moved lower, sliding between her legs. For a moment Kate's body stiffened in resistance but then her instincts kicked in and she relaxed, opening herself joyfully to his exploratory caresses.

'Do you like that?' Kate moaned and pushed against his hand. 'And that...?' he persisted, reaching deeper inside her.

Kate gasped, eyelids lifted to reveal her dark passion-glazed stare. 'I don't *like* anything you do,' she told him. 'I *love* it! I love the way you look, I love the way you sound, I love your smell and most of all I love what you do to me!' she cried.

He kissed her then with a deep, drowning desperation that fired her blood. Lips still attached to his, Kate began to rip at his clothes with feverish haste as she looped one long leg across his thigh.

'Did I mention that you're absolutely the most beautiful thing I've ever seen?' she gasped as he stopped kissing her—*which was bad*—to assist her frantic efforts to undress him—*which was good!* 'The bits that I've seen, anyhow.'

Javier laughed, a low husky sound that sent shivers of hot anticipation curling down her spine.

When she got to see the rest, Kate got a lot less vocal. She felt weak with lust and longing as she hungrily absorbed the rippling strength of his long, lean, tightly muscled body as he knelt between her legs. She knew the mind-blowingly erotic image of his golden body, with its strategic drifts of dark body hair, glistening with need for her, would never fade from her mind.

'What's the verdict?'

Kate dragged her eyes upwards. He had room to sound confident; he really was nothing short of spectacular!

'Don't talk,' she begged, her voice thickening emotionally as she reached for him.

Javier's eyes darkened dramatically as he came down to her, brushing the rosy tips of her trembling breasts with his tongue before sliding down lower over her body.

Back arched, Kate cried out and pushed up towards him, moaning his name, her fingers tangled in his dark hair.

He licked his way back up to her face, reducing Kate to a mindless, mass of inarticulate craving somewhere along the way.

Eyes closed tight, she felt him kiss her paper-thin fluttering lids. A long soundless gasp of anticipation escaped her lips as he parted her legs.

His tongue plunged into her mouth at the same moment he plunged into her body, sheathing himself deeply in her tight, hot wetness.

'You hold me so tight,' he whispered against her ear.

Her body clenched around him. 'Oh, God, Javier!' she gasped brokenly, nipping frantically at his neck and shoulders with her teeth. His face above her was a mask of dark, primitive need that fuelled the raw urgency coursing through her blood.

'Please,' she breathed into his mouth and he thrust carefully into her. *'Harder…!'*

Her ragged plea had an electrifying effect upon him.

Later, as she lay there, her body throbbing with contentment, Kate recalled with a bemused smile the moment something inside her had recognised and instinctively responded to the savagery in his wild possession.

While the sweat cooled on their bodies, she lay there in the darkness, stroking Javier's dark head as it lay nestled between her breasts. She was still awake when he awoke hours later and turned once more to her.

His lovemaking was less urgent but no less sweet the second time and if anything her release, because he delayed it so long, was even more shattering. Afterwards she did sleep and when she awoke it was light and she was alone.

She didn't cry; crying would have been some sort of release and Kate couldn't find that. She doubted she ever would.

CHAPTER ELEVEN

THE head of Chambers, a normally morose character, was quite animated when he came across to their table to personally congratulate Kate on the way she'd handled the Benton case.

Kate smiled uncomfortably as she listened to the glowing comments he made about the combination of inspiration and dedication embodied in her attitude that was making her such an extremely valuable member of the team.

'Another bottle of bubbly, I think,' her date for the night cried as the older man returned to his own table. He lifted his glass to Kate, unable to prevent a shade of jealousy creeping into his bright toast. 'Who's a clever girl, then? Quite the teacher's pet.'

'It was a bit over the top, wasn't it? I expect he's had a bit too much to drink.' She smiled, trying to play down the incident. She was well aware that Ian's competitive nature resented her recent successes.

In truth she felt a bit of a fake, receiving the praise; it was not dedication or a desire to outshine her contemporaries that had made her throw herself body and soul into her work, but a need to fill the hours.

In theory, since she arrived at the office long before everyone else and left her desk long after everyone else, usually piled high with briefs, she shouldn't have been left with any time to think. Unfortunately the great yawning gap between theory and practice meant that no matter how hard she worked or how exhausted she was when she fell into bed, Javier was never very far from her thoughts at any time.

The most ridiculous things reminded her of him. She'd never noticed before how many unusually tall men there were in London; as for Spanish accents, she couldn't catch a bus or the Tube without hearing one…! Not that any of them had possessed Javier's incredible velvet drawl.

When one of the secretaries had returned from her holiday in Majorca, waxing lyrical about her experiences there, it had taken Kate half an hour locked in the ladies' room to compose herself…and night time was definitely the worst. Then the memories crowded in, leaving her to toss and turn restlessly all night.

Fortunately her red eyes that afternoon had gone unnoticed, as did the fact she had returned from Majorca a different person to the one who had left. Kate felt sure the very deep differences she felt inside must be mirrored on her face, but amazingly the only thing anyone had commented on was the fact she'd begun to wear her contact lenses almost full time.

'No, can't blame it on the booze,' her date contradicted. 'Sampson's a Quaker, teetotal.'

'Not for me, thanks, Ian.' Kate smiled, quickly placing her hand over her half-full glass.

Though normally an undemanding and entertaining companion, when he had had too much to drink, as he had now, Ian tended to become loud and sulky; neither quality endeared him to Kate. Ian was a barrister, as were most of the other people at the glittering charity gathering organised by the Law Society. It was late and there was an atmosphere of general jollity. They'd been fed well, they'd endured the inevitable speeches from luminaries; now they were all eager to party and Ian was more eager than most.

'Don't be a wet blanket, Katie,' he slurred. 'You haven't had a drop all night.'

Sandy, sitting opposite Kate threw her friend a sympathetic look. Though she hadn't said anything, Kate thought maybe Sandy had her own suspicions about why she was avoiding alcohol.

'I'll have some of that, thanks, Ian,' she cried cheerfully, pushing her own glass towards him. 'I think old Sampson must be worried about you being headhunted, Kate.'

Though Sandy's actions achieved the desired purpose of distracting Ian from his determination to fill Kate's glass, they didn't improve his disposition.

'Then the rumours are true, you have had an offer from Hargreaves and St John!' he exclaimed with a scowl. 'Must be a big help to climb the greasy pole when Daddy's there to put a word or two in the right ear,' he reflected bitterly.

'Out of order, Ian, old boy,' the man beside him said quietly. 'Kate is a damned good advocate and you know it.'

The sound of the placid old Etonian drawl acted like a red rag to a bull on Ian in his present ugly mood. 'Shove it, Toby, *old boy!*' he snarled, his complexion deepening to an unattractive red.

Kate was relieved by the fresh distraction afforded when the two women who'd been missing from the table retook their seats. They both looked animated.

'You'll never guess who we've just seen…!' one cried.

'I'm only guessing if you narrow the odds,' Kate responded. 'Give us a clue—actress, politician, royalty…?'

'Not a *she,* a *he.*'

'The sort of man you'd find in the ladies' loo…?' Kate pretended to think hard. 'That doesn't narrow the odds much,' she complained and everyone laughed.

'We didn't see him in the loo, he was just coming in with the minister of…you know, the politician that wrote that thriller.'

'Now that narrows the odds even less,' Toby reflected drily. 'Your lack of political awareness is staggering, darling,' he continued smoothly drawing his pretty partner to her feet and dragging her towards the dance floor.

'Go on,' Sandy urged the remaining talebearer, once the couple were gone, 'tell us who this exciting person is before you implode. My money's on let me see...Brad Pitt...' she decided with a lascivious smile.

'Optimist,' Kate chuckled.

'Much better than that,' came the smug response. 'Oh, God, I don't believe it...' she gasped suddenly, her face going pale. 'Don't look now, but I think...yes,' she hissed, 'he's coming over here!'

'Dance with me, Kate,' Ian, who had been watching with a scowl as Toby smooched across the floor gracefully with his pretty girlfriend, said abruptly. 'That idiot really loves himself, doesn't he?' he brooded irritably to nobody in particular.

'Thanks, Ian, but I'm not really in the mood...' Not anxious to inflame the situation, Kate softened her refusal with a smile.

His eyes still on Toby, Ian rose unsteadily from his chair. 'I'll get you in the mood,' he boasted aggressively, grabbing Kate's wrist.

'I really don't want to dance, Ian,' Kate insisted, trying to pull her hand free from his grip.

Being breathed on by someone whose breath was forty per cent proof was not her idea of fun, and she wouldn't have put it past Ian in his present mood to pick a fight with Toby on the dance floor. She was deeply regretting accepting his invitation, if 'we might as well go together' could be termed as such. These occasions could be awkward if you went solo.

'Of course you do...'

A voice of steel and ice from behind Kate softly contradicted this sulky claim.

'The lady does not wish to dance with you.'

Kate froze, all the colour rushing from her face, only to be replaced seconds later by a flood of colour. Her heart was pounding so hard she could hardly hear her own jumbled thoughts.

An irritated snarl on his face, Ian spun around. Under normal circumstances, his sense of self-preservation would have been immediately activated by the size and character of his adversary, but the alcohol in his veins made him reluctant to back down. Drunk or not, though, he couldn't hold that scornful shimmering blue gaze for more than a nanosecond.

'What's it to you...?'

Kate deliberately didn't make the same mistake as Ian and look at the intruder. Choice didn't enter into the decision; she simply didn't trust her body not to betray her in some weak shameful way if she permitted it a glimpse of what it had been too long starved of. His voice, the faint familiar scent of his cologne that made her nostrils flare was already doing some very alarming things to her nervous system. Any second now someone was going to notice she was shaking like a leaf. What unkind twist of fate had brought him here tonight...?

'Ian, leave it,' Kate breathed urgently. In considerable agitation she rose unsteadily to her feet. She forced her lips to smile and clutched the table with her free hand for support. 'Leave it alone; I'll dance with you.'

Still she didn't look at him. She was desperately trying to compose her traumatised thoughts.

Think...think... As tempting as the idea was, she couldn't follow her first impulse and hide under the table—up and coming barristers in slinky strapless ball gowns did not scrabble about on the floor without exciting unwanted attention. No, somehow she had to deal with the fact this wasn't one of her fantasies; Javier really was here in the flesh... *Don't think flesh, Katie!*

Her resolve weakened and she couldn't resist the over-powering desire to turn her head and risked a furtive peek from under her lashes—the pit of her stomach vanished into a black hole. Caution and self-respect forgotten, she stared hungrily.

He looked exactly how she remembered, only *more…!*

Six feet four inches of mouthwateringly delicious, rampant masculinity. Moreover, he looked perfectly at home in his surroundings and supremely, shockingly sexy in a dark, well-cut evening jacket.

Kate hardly wondered at the awed, open-mouthed silence around the table or the intense level of interest his presence was arousing. A tall, elegant, outrageously *male* figure projecting an effortless air of cool command that was at sharp variance to the younger man's truculent aggression, Javier was always going to attract buckets of attention.

As if he felt her scrutiny, his sapphire gaze suddenly swivelled towards her. The room and everyone in it disappeared as his eyes moved over her face, as if he was memorising every curve. At some subconscious level she registered the ripple as his throat muscles moved convulsively, a deep sigh that juddered through his tense frame.

'You will not dance with this man, Kate,' he stated emphatically.

As if her obedience was something he took for granted—some things didn't change—he immediately switched his attention back to the younger man. His narrowed eyes moved to the hand still curved around her wrist. 'Let her go,' he purred softly.

'*Says who…?*'

Kate, who had seen the menacing expression in Javier's eyes, decided Ian was a lot more stupid than he looked!

In reply, Javier's hand closed around Ian's own wrist and the younger man paled as his fingers opened in response to the steely pressure. He swore.

'You will dance with me!' Javier decreed autocratically.

Kate's jaw dropped, even for Javier this was over the top! 'Your wish is my command and all that...' she breathed shakily.

A humiliated Ian jumped in before Javier could respond to her caustic jibe. 'Who the hell do you think you are, waltzing in here trying to pinch my girlfriend?'

The danger lurking just beneath the elegant façade of Javier's silken smile, the barely suppressed fury in his expression, finally penetrated even Ian's drunken bravado. The younger man instinctively drew back.

'Boyfriend?' One dark brow rose to an incredulous angle. 'I suppose we are all permitted errors of judgement occasionally,' he acknowledged directing a glance of dismissive scorn towards Ian. 'As for who I am...' he began forcefully...

Kate gave a horrified gasp, suddenly sure this explanation wasn't going to stop at his name.

'You're Javier Montero!' Toby, who chose that moment to wander back to the table with his girlfriend, exclaimed. 'Worth a bundle,' he elaborated to a pale-looking Ian. 'Several bundles, actually. If you ever need a good legal brain...? The name's Toby Challoner,' he grinned, pumping Javier's hand with friendly fervour.

A flicker of amusement crossed Javier's taut features. 'I'll keep that in mind,' he promised, before turning his attention to Kate, who was experiencing the bizarre sensation of her two separate worlds colliding.

She looked at his hand, stretched out towards her, and was seized by an overwhelming compulsion to meet it halfway. Not one to submit without a struggle to inevitability, she tucked her tingling fingertips behind her back.

'I don't care who he is. He can't dance with you, Kate.'

'For God's sake, Ian, shut up!' she flared, exasperated by his feeble chest-beating. In fact, she was tired full stop of being told what to do by men! 'I'll dance with whoever I want to.'

'And you want to dance with me, Kate?' Javier suggested, tilting her chin with one finger. 'I can't believe we have never danced together, *querida.*'

The gasp around the table was audible.

'And I can't believe you're here doing this to me, Javier,' she responded hoarsely.

And, other than the fact he enjoyed any opportunity to throw his weight around, she couldn't see *why* he was here now…unless…? Did he want a divorce…? she wondered despondently.

'He knows our Katie!' Toby boomed good-naturedly. 'Kept that quiet, sweet girl.'

'Sort of,' Kate replied vaguely as she felt the pressure of Javier's strong fingers close about her own.

Javier, his dark head imperiously high, drew her to his side. '*Sort of* as in Kate is my wife,' he announced, bestowing a hawkish smile of blinding brilliance upon his stunned audience.

The image left in Kate's mind as she was dragged off was Ian's sickly pale expression of shock.

'*Oh, my God!*' she groaned over and over as he drew her inexorably towards the crowded dance floor. 'What are you trying to do?'

'Avoid your toes. Listen to the music, *querida.*'

'What are you doing here, Javier? Were you just in town and you thought, what the hell, I've nothing better to do, I'll go and ruin Kate's life…that should be good for a laugh!'

'I am not laughing.'

Indeed he wasn't; his eyes were fixed with uncompromising solemnity on her flushed, upturned features.

'If you're after a quickie divorce, you couldn't have chosen a worse way to ensure my co-operation,' she warned him grimly. 'A simple letter from your solicitor would have done. Right now, I'm feeling particularly vicious!'

His sombre expression momentarily softened. 'You haven't got a malicious or vindictive bone in your body.'

Kate found his confidence was deeply frustrating.

'Don't you understand? Now everyone will *know!*' She lifted her horrified eyes to his dark face as her body began to respond automatically to the gentle rhythm and Javier's light, guiding touch. They flowed together like honey, moving as one fluid unit.

A stab of sexual longing of paralysing intensity lanced through her body. Helpless to control what was happening to her, Kate felt her starved senses react with pathetic predictability to his closeness; they drank in eagerly the unique fragrance of him and revelled in the hard-muscled male angularity of his lean body.

A judicious application of pressure from his fingers played across the hollow at the base of her spine brought her in close contact with his thighs; the resulting flicker of shock in her wide eyes as she felt his unashamed arousal made him smile with bold brilliance down at her.

'I can see it might limit your social life somewhat,' he admitted with a thin-lipped smile. 'A certain type of man is attracted by the forbidden pleasures a married woman's bed offers but I don't think your admirer is one of them. He looked a little unwell, I thought...'

This display of smug hypocrisy made Kate momentarily loose her footing. She doubted very much if Javier had been broadcasting his unavailability amongst the eligible highborn Spanish lovelies who had been no doubt falling over each other in their eagerness to offer him comfort. The thought of it made her feel physically sick.

'Even if Ian was my boyfriend, which he isn't, it wouldn't be any of your business.'

'I'm making it my business,' he revealed calmly. His scrutiny was unbearably penetrating as he scanned her face hungrily. 'You look very beautiful tonight, *querida*,' he continued seamlessly as Kate blinked back up at him in stunned disbelief.

'So do you,' she admitted wistfully, without thinking. 'What do you mean, *your business?*' she puzzled in a troubled whisper.

'I mean that marrying in haste…'

'And for all the wrong reasons.'

'As you say,' he conceded impatiently. 'It doesn't make the pledges we made any less binding.'

'Since when?' A dark shadow of anguish crossed her face. 'You're the one who walked away from me.' An experience Kate knew she could only bear once in a lifetime.

'You have no idea how hard that was for me, but I thought it was what you wanted. I thought you wanted your life I had stolen back.'

'It is what I want,' she replied in small defiant voice.

'I was a fool!' He appeared oblivious to the curious looks his loud, bitter pronouncement had drawn.

'Did you come here about the divorce…?'

His laugh almost hurt to hear.

With no warning Javier stopped dead in the middle of the dancing couples who diverted curiously around the motionless pair. He closed his eyes and his head fell back. Kate watched with growing bewilderment as the muscles in his brown throat worked convulsively.

'I missed you.'

Kate firmly doused the flare of hope that fluttered in her breast and shook her head stubbornly. 'I don't believe you.' She *couldn't*, not knowing how much being wrong would hurt.

His head jerked upright, the fan of dark lashes lifted from his cheekbones revealing an expression of implacable determination. His powerful chest expanded and his shoulders firmed as if he was marshalling all his not inconsiderable authority.

'Let me convince you.'

For the first time Kate noticed the tell-tale signs of quivering tension in his body. The nerve throbbing in his lean cheek. The extra sharp edge to the jutting angularity of his facial bones.

'You've lost weight,' she observed in a distracted, worried manner.

His body, always greyhound lean, had an even more spare look to it. This lean, hungry look was probably connected to the combustible, dangerous aura he was exuding. He looked like someone who had been sustained on adrenaline and will power alone for too long.

Probably the stress of his grandfather's death, and the extra responsibilities that had fallen on his broad shoulders were responsible for these changes. Plus making sure that Luis Gonzalez finally got his comeuppance. Kate felt indignant that nobody close to him had had the good sense to see he needed taking care of. She contemplated the pleasure it would give her to give them a piece of her mind, were she really his wife and in a position to do so.

A wistful expression made her soft mouth quiver.

Of course, if she had been his wife in a real sense, there wouldn't be any need for anyone else to make sure he didn't push himself too hard; she could have done that herself.

He gave a dismissive shrug, displaying an infuriatingly cavalier attitude to his health.

'Everyone has their limits, Javier, even you,' she remonstrated.

He gave an odd laugh. 'If I didn't know that, the past six weeks taught me that and many things I didn't know before.'

Her eyes darkened. 'Has it been very bad...?' Her concern increased as she noted the faint sheen of perspiration gleaming on his vibrant, golden skin. Kate, who had seen him appear cool and collected on occasions when the temperature had reached the high thirties, knew that Javier was totally impervious to the heat.

'*Hell!*' came the succinct response. 'Are you seeing anyone?' The words emerged from between clenched white teeth.

Her round chin firmed. 'And if I was?' some perverse imp impelled her to respond.

A white line appeared around his compressed lips. Kate had never seen the veneer of sophistication that covered his passionate nature thinner. Only pride prevented her from revealing how shaken she felt by the raw emotions spilling from him.

'*Por Dios,* do not trifle with me, Kate. I am not *safe!*' he confided, breathing hard as he fought to retain his shredded self-control.

Shaken to the core by his raw pronouncement, Kate had no intention of testing the authenticity of this claim.

She cleared her bone-dry throat.

'No, I'm not seeing anyone, Javier. I think,' she hypothesised, exposing her inner soul to him with a rush of relief, 'that it's likely you've spoilt me for any other man.'

When Kate finally worked up the courage to look at him, her bruised, aching heart stilled and then soared at the expression of tender triumph she encountered on his devastatingly handsome face. Even at that moment she hardly dared trust her interpretation of his expression.

'That is as it should be, *mi esposa,* for there is no doubt that you have spoilt me for any other woman. I think I fell in love with you that very first moment I saw you. I didn't realise it until you fainted outside the church. I was overwhelmed by my selfishness; I was sure you must despise me. Like a fool I let you go…I was too afraid of rejection to ask you to stay with me, but now as you see my pride is in tatters.'

'Not so as you'd notice,' Kate breathed with a delirious laugh as she gazed transfixed into his stunningly handsome face. Wonderingly, she lifted her small hand to his bronzed cheek; Javier murmured her name as he turned his head and pressed a fervent kiss to her open palm.

Kate's tummy muscles quivered violently as she gazed at his dark glossy head.

'I don't believe this is real.' She bit her lip, struggling to hold back the emotional tears. If she started crying, she feared she wouldn't be able to stop. 'I've dreamed so often about this moment, but I never thought it would happen…'

Javier gazed with fierce pride into her luminous eyes. 'I think I might just know a way of convincing you.'

Kate responded body and soul to the demands of his burning kiss which only ended when they both registered the polite 'Wouldn't disturb you for the world!'

'Toby, isn't it…?' Javier responded with only slightly less cool assurance than usual.

'Thing is, I thought you might like to know the music stopped playing about five minutes ago, and not to put too fine a point on it,' he glanced sympathetically at Kate's fiery cheeks and cleared his throat, 'you are the floor show.'

'Oh, God…!' Kate moaned, suddenly conscious they were standing quite alone in the middle of the large dance floor, the focus of several hundred pairs of curious eyes.

'There is no shame involved in kissing your husband, *mi esposa*,' Javier reproached, surveying the room with a staggering display of supreme indifference which Kate deeply envied.

'Blame it on my British inhibitions,' she gritted cringing at the thought of the spectacle she must have presented.

A gleam appeared in his fabulous densely lashed eyes. 'I had not noticed you had any.'

Kate choked and shot a glance towards Toby, who was tactfully examining his fingernails. 'For God's sake, Javier!' she reproached, a laugh quivering in her throat.

Javier smiled complacently down into her deliciously flushed face before turning politely to the young lawyer.

'We are indebted to you, Toby,' he said smoothly as he inclined his head towards the loose-limbed younger man. 'Do you speak Spanish?' he asked abruptly.

The other man looked startled. 'Pretty well; appalling accent though,' he admitted with a self-deprecating grin.

'Well, if you were serious about work, ring this number,' he said in an off-hand manner as he handed the startled young man a card.

'*Are you serious…?*'

'Always where business is concerned,' Javier responded with a wolfish grin. 'Now, if you'll excuse us, Kate and I were just leaving.'

'Good of you to tell me,' she murmured as he drew her to his side.

One dark eyebrow rose to a satanic angle. 'You prefer we continue our conversation here?'

'We weren't talking.'

'That is why I thought it would be wiser to adjourn to somewhere less public. I have an overwhelming desire to make love to my wife, you see,' he explained, with a contemplative smile that sent a sharp thrill of sexual desire through her.

'In that case,' she responded huskily, 'lead the way.'

Kate gave a sigh of relief as they finally reached the porticoed exit. She had tried to emulate her husband's splendid indifference to the stares and whispers that had dogged their progress, but it hadn't been easy. As for Javier, he hadn't been much help; his reserves of tolerance had quickly worn thin when people with the slightest claim to his acquaintance repeatedly approached them. Towards the end, his methods of ridding himself of those unwise enough to impede their progress were brutally abrupt enough to make Kate cringe.

'Being rich and important is no excuse for bad manners.'

He immediately accepted culpability. 'I know, but I am desperate to make love to you, *mi esposa.*'

Kate was quick to recognise that these were extenuating circumstances.

'You think I'm a pushover, don't you?' she accused as she happily allowed him to draw her into his arms.

'I think you are the sweetest, most enchanting little witch in the world,' he told her throatily.

'Well, I suppose you have your good points; you were pretty nice to Toby,' she admitted.

'No, I was not *nice* to Toby. I rely on first impressions and my first impression of him tells me he is loyal but not afraid of speaking his mind. People like that are surprisingly rare.'

'So your first impressions are always right, are they?' She widened her eyes innocently. 'What about your first impressions of me?' She looked up at him, her eyes dancing with bright laughing expectancy.

'Oh, my first impressions of you were one hundred per cent correct,' he assured her.

Recalling some of his less than flattering accusations at the time, Kate's eyes widened indignantly.

'I knew you were trouble, even then.'

Trouble…? Kate liked the sound of that; it made her feel bold and dangerous, a real femme fatale.

'You'd better believe it,' she purred, giving a provocative little wriggle.

Delighted to see his eyes darken responsively to the light-hearted provocation, Kate was winding her arms around his neck when she was blinded by a series of bright camera flashes. Javier immediately moved to block her from the view of the opportunist photographer.

He moved swiftly but even when she was in the back of the chauffeur-driven limousine which had pulled up in front of the building the photographer, his camera pressed up against the glass, was still popping away.

Javier, white-faced with anger, gave his instructions to the driver before pressing the button that brought down the smoked glass screen between them.

'Does that happen to you often?' Kate asked, sinking back into the luxurious upholstery with a sigh.

'I'm afraid it does.' He regarded her pale, distressed features with concern. 'I'm sorry, *querida,* for exposing you to that, but someone inside must have contacted the press about our rather public display. I should have anticipated it.' He frowned.

'It wasn't very nice,' she admitted candidly. 'And I expect seeing myself looking like some cross-eyed sheep in some scummy paper tomorrow won't be nice either, but I suppose I'd better get used to it,' she returned with a philosophical shrug. 'That is, if you're serious about wanting this marriage to be for real…?'

Javier's tense anxious look was replaced by one of wondering appreciation. 'You know something, you are quite incredible. You do realise that as my wife you won't have the luxury of anonymity any longer?'

'To be your wife,' she admitted shyly, 'I'm willing to put up with a good deal.'

A look of fierce joy flared in his eyes as, with a sharp intake of breath, he gathered her soft yielding body close. 'I am the luckiest man on earth.'

Kate emerged breathless and dishevelled from the crushing embrace.

Javier leaned back in his seat and loosened his tie. 'Com-

bining your career and marriage will not be easy,' he observed, watching her face carefully as he smoothed down
his own rumpled hair. 'You will often have to deal with
conflicting demands upon your time.'

Was he asking her to give up her career, was that what
the wife of a Montero was expected to do…? Perhaps she
had been naïve not to see this coming.

'Are you asking me to choose between you and my job?'
she asked him bluntly.

'What do you take me for?' he demanded in a tone of
deep affront. 'You think that I respect what you have
achieved so little, I would ask to throw it away, so that you
can be at my beck and call?' He reached out for her and
curving his hand over the back of her head drew her face
to within an inch of his.

Kate's head spun dizzily.

'I would not try and destroy all the things that make you
the woman I love.' His electric blue eyes swept over her
face. 'You are courageous, often terrifyingly so…' he
mused darkly. 'And funny, of course,' he added, sliding his
fingers through her silky hair. 'Bright, infuriating and stubborn. You think you know better than me and say so, which
I admit is good for me…'

'I'm going to remind you that you said that,' Kate promised huskily.

'I used to think I wanted a woman who needed me to
shelter her from the harsh things in life…'

'Sarah…'

Javier nodded ruefully. 'That would have been a total
disaster,' he confessed, shaking his head. 'Her vulnerability, it touched me deeply. Please do not laugh,' he added,
an uncomfortable slash of embarrassed colour appearing
along his cheekbones. 'I think I saw myself as some sort
of gallant white knight. She didn't need a knight or a social

worker, just a man who loved her, and she was wise enough
to recognise him straight away.'

Kate felt a lot happier with the nagging Sarah question
disposed of—there was now only one unresolved
issue…and how he was going to take that she didn't know.

'I might need saving occasionally, and if not I've heard
that role-playing can be very stimulating,' she observed
cheekily.

Javier's rich laughter rang out. 'Meeting you has taught
me that it is very much more exciting to have a mate who
can constantly surprise me. Of course you must continue
your work,' he insisted. 'It will require some adjustments…' he continued absently as he began to nuzzle her
sensitive earlobe. 'You have no idea how much I've missed
you…' he rasped throatily. 'So many times something happened and I thought, I must tell Kate, only to remember
you were hundreds of miles away. I picked up the phone
so many times, when desperate to hear your voice…it was
only stubborn pride that stopped me dialling your number…'

Despite the delicious shivers chasing up and down her
spine and the desire coursing sweetly through her blood,
Kate gently pulled away. It wasn't easy; she was so sensitive to him, all he had to do was look at her and she
melted.

She had to tell him now.

She cleared her throat; Javier was looking at her warily.
Her love for him was like an aching knot behind her breast
bone. She wondered how he was going to be looking at her
in a few minutes.

'Actually, Javier…'

'Mi esposa…?' He cupped her chin in his hand and studied her troubled face. 'What is worrying you?'

'Those adjustments you were talking about, it might require a few more than you think,' she admitted apologetically.

'How so…?'

'Well, you know how I wasn't superstitious…'

The colour drained dramatically from his face. He shook his head. 'You don't mean…?' he gasped.

Kate nodded. 'Yup!' she breezed with a levity she was far from feeling. 'I did two tests just in case I was wrong, but yes, I'm definitely pregnant.'

Worryingly, his expression didn't alter at all.

'And you feel…?'

'Sick as a dog in this morning,' she admitted. 'And I can't stand the smell of coffee, but other than that…'

'I mean, how do you *feel?*'

'Well, I've never actually fancied myself as the maternal type…' Looking down at her flat belly with an expression of wonder, she didn't see the flicker of despair cross his face. 'But once the shock wore off I danced around the bedroom like an idiot,' she revealed, pressing a protective hand across her tummy. 'I'm tickled pink, over the moon and prone to violent tearful outbursts, one of which I feel coming on now,' she confessed. 'Of course, I don't expect you to feel the same way…'

'Feel the same way?' he exclaimed, running his hands down her bare arms before taking both her hands in his. He lifted them to his lips. 'There was never any question of how *I* feel. How could I not be delighted that the woman I love is carrying my child?' he asked her incredulously. 'It was your feelings that I was worried about. I thought you might resent having motherhood thrust upon you because of my carelessness.' His stern frown held self-reproach. 'It was criminally irresponsible.'

'Hey, I was there too, remember! I don't recall fighting you off with a stick. I enjoyed making this baby…'

Her defiance brought an amused glitter to his eyes. 'I

think someone in the outer Hebrides might not have heard that, *querida*.' His eyes softened tenderly. 'I enjoyed making him too.'

'As far as I'm concerned, Javier, this is a very wanted pregnancy. In fact, there's only one more thing worrying me...'

'What is that?'

A little encouragement, she decided, looking lovingly into the face of her husband, would not go amiss. 'When are you going to get criminally irresponsible again?'

'I am yours to command,' he told her with a smile.

Now that opened up all sorts of interesting possibilities. 'Are you sure you know what you're letting yourself in for...?'

'Forty years of being under your delicious thumb?' he suggested hopefully as he drew the digit under discussion into his mouth.

'I wouldn't mind too terribly if you were on top occasionally,' she admitted, darting him a sultry look from under the shade of her lashes.

'Well, variety, so I hear, is the spice of life.'

Kate, giving herself up wholeheartedly to his kiss, was smugly confident she'd have plenty of that with Javier!

HARLEQUIN *Presents*

Welcome to a world filled with passion, romance and royals!

Royal Brides

The Scorsolini Princes: Proud rulers and passionate lovers who need convenient wives!

HIS ROYAL LOVE-CHILD

by Lucy Monroe

June 2006

Danette Michaels knew that there
would be no marriage or future as Principe Marcello
Scorsolini's secret mistress. When she wanted more, the affair
ended. Until a pregnancy test changed everything...

Other titles from this new trilogy by Lucy Monroe
THE PRINCE'S VIRGIN WIFE—May
THE SCORSOLINI MARRIAGE BARGAIN—July

---

www.eHarlequin.com   HPRB0606

HARLEQUIN *Presents*

Royal Brides

**The Scorsolini Princes:
proud rulers and passionate lovers
who need convenient wives!**

Welcome to this brand-new miniseries,
set in glamorous and exotic places—it's
a world filled with passion, romance and royals!

Don't miss this new trilogy by

Lucy Monroe

THE PRINCE'S VIRGIN WIFE
May 2006

HIS ROYAL LOVE-CHILD
June 2006

THE SCORSOLINI MARRIAGE BARGAIN
July 2006

If you enjoyed what you just read,
then we've got an offer you can't resist!

Take 2 bestselling
love stories FREE!

Plus get a FREE surprise gift!

Clip this page and mail it to Harlequin Reader Service®

IN U.S.A.	IN CANADA
3010 Walden Ave.	P.O. Box 609
P.O. Box 1867	Fort Erie, Ontario
Buffalo, N.Y. 14240-1867	L2A 5X3

YES! Please send me 2 free Harlequin Presents® novels and my free surprise gift. After receiving them, if I don't wish to receive anymore, I can return the shipping statement marked cancel. If I don't cancel, I will receive 6 brand-new novels every month, before they're available in stores! In the U.S.A., bill me at the bargain price of $3.80 plus 25¢ shipping & handling per book and applicable sales tax, if any*. In Canada, bill me at the bargain price of $4.47 plus 25¢ shipping & handling per book and applicable taxes**. That's the complete price and a savings of at least 10% off the cover prices—what a great deal! I understand that accepting the 2 free books and gift places me under no obligation ever to buy any books. I can always return a shipment and cancel at any time. Even if I never buy another book from Harlequin, the 2 free books and gift are mine to keep forever.

106 HDN DZ7Y
306 HDN DZ7Z

Name	(PLEASE PRINT)	
Address	Apt.#	
City	State/Prov.	Zip/Postal Code

Not valid to current Harlequin Presents® subscribers.

Want to try two free books from another series?
Call 1-800-873-8635 or visit www.morefreebooks.com.

* Terms and prices subject to change without notice. Sales tax applicable in N.Y.
** Canadian residents will be charged applicable provincial taxes and GST.
All orders subject to approval. Offer limited to one per household.
® are registered trademarks owned and used by the trademark owner and or its licensee.

PRES04R   ©2004 Harlequin Enterprises Limited

HARLEQUIN® Presents®

Bedded by Blackmail

Forced to bed...then to wed?

He's got her firmly in his sights
and she has only one chance of
survival—surrender to
his blackmail...and
him...in his bed!

THE ITALIAN'S
BLACKMAILED
MISTRESS

by

Jacqueline Baird

On sale this June!